UNDER THE TREES, EATEN

UNDER THE TREES, EATEN

ADAM RIGGIO

BLANKSPACE PUBLICATIONS

Under the Trees, Eaten

Edited by Jeffrey D. Douglas, Patrick Casey and Dave Boylan. Cover design and layout by Jeffrey D. Douglas. No portion of this book, except in compliance with fair use laws, may be copied without written permission. All characters and events in this book are fictional. Any semblance to reality is coincidence.

Cover image by Kayte Hachey.
Author photo by Matt Schneider.

ISBN 978-0-9938111-0-4

First Edition, September 2014.

Manufactured in the USA through BlankSpace Publications.
131 Thornton Avenue
London, Ontario
N5Y 2Y6

BlankSpace Publications
www.blankspacep.com

Library and Archives Canada Cataloguing in Publication

Riggio, Adam, 1983-, author
        Under the trees, eaten / Adam Riggio.

ISBN 978-0-9938111-0-4 (pbk.)

        I. Title.

PS8635.I534U53 2014   C813'.6   C2014-903530-6

…'punishment' is what revenge calls itself; with a lying word it hypocritically asserts its good conscience.

—Friedrich Nietzsche, "On Redemption," *Thus Spoke Zarathustra*

Pre.

Just a few minutes ago I was in daylight, in the forest. Then there was the sound, a clicking, like tapshoes dancing across a wooden floor. The sound was irregular, rising and falling in strange periods and meters and coming at me from all directions. The clicking drifted through trees, bushes, underbrush, following me into the cave mouth. Then darkness.

No human feet could move with a pattern like that.

There's the sound again, tapshoes on wood, an irregular tempo rising and falling in strange patterns. But the ground and walls are pliant, billowing like an engorged blister around the contours of my hands and feet as my flesh sinks into a flesh that's darkness also. Searching for memory here turns up emptiness. There must be something to remember. Remember their voices. They were calling for you to find them, two voices entangled as one. One fell thousands of feet into the forest, exploded and burned until there was nothing but gray dust. There are flowers growing there now, and impossible insects with three jaws. And there was light.

Light has no home here. Light should banish darkness. This darkness swallows light.

Are there still legs? Legs are moving a body deeper into the chasm, drawn forward beyond the reach of my control.

My? What could I have had?

Darkness can be seen and touched, feels like infinitely flexible sheets of wispy fabric waving in breezes of still air. It wraps its umbral curtains around whatever enters, folding bodies inside itself.

Just a few days ago there was light, heat, sweat beading on a forehead and the most beautifully impossible monsters. Just a few seconds ago I heard a scream for help, several screams entangled as one, a scream from the dead.

I haven't been aware of myself for a long time.

And now the sound comes with the darkness again, clicking that grows louder and faster, the only marker of the flow of time. How much time has passed?

Past?

A thousand tapshoes on hollow wood in a cave where the ground is an amniotic sac. Darkness spills into the grooves of my flesh, filling every pore with a substance rigid as bone and supple as curdling blood. The sensation is one of drowning, but drowning requires a body. There is no body now. There is only the scream.

1.

My father died at 70, which I suppose was long enough to live. But it would have been longer if it wasn't for the search. Most of the people here are his friends from the seniors' center. I started taking him there when he could have been called a young man at the center, only 62, just so that he'd spend a couple of hours a day doing something other than poring over airplane technical manuals and forensic reports. Even so, the last time he had gone there was three years ago. Quite a few are older than he was, some by more than a decade. There are also his old friends to deal with, the ones whose lives he dropped out of, who I never really knew. I keep an eye on these unfamiliar faces to make sure they don't approach me with a view to ask questions.

"You visited my place in Connecticut once, and you just ran around my backyard." An old man with cement-gray hair is sitting next to me, telling a story, trying to sympathize. He's a young old man, like dad once was. He's muscular, but carries a cane, which I can't help but find a little strange, though mostly I just want him to shut up. "I still remember you chasing Paul around and around. It started with you chasing my old dog Simone, then Paul tried to catch you to come inside for dinner, then the dog started chasing him, then I lost track of it all!" I've gotten tired very quickly of hearing that melancholy laughter of old men who suspect that they've started to lose their reasons for laughing.

In what I guess most people would find normal circumstances, I might be intrigued to hear stories about who my father was before I was born, or even before he met my mother. I suppose that's what most people think funerals are for, telling stories to resurrect ghosts and memories. "All six of us came back to his apartment and because the storm had come up so suddenly while we were at the bar, everything was covered in ice. None of us are wearing proper winter boots." A woman in her mid-sixties is speaking to me now. "And he slips and falls flat on his back with his hand still on the key, so it snaps off in the front door lock. I don't think anyone could use the main door to the apartment building for at least a week! So he's scaling the fire escape to reach his back door like he's a mountain goat!"

At thirty-two years old, I'm the youngest person here. This crowd should've been much older, as dad's funeral should not have been for another decade. Their stories all seem so strange, a different person from the man I've called my father for the last fifteen years. The man in all their stories is smiling. "I know it's awkward to ask, but Paul never talked about your mother." This is a friend from the seniors' center speaking, hesitating, coughing. I don't want to answer the question, so I mumble something about her having died a long time ago. She understands that I won't talk about Zoiey in any detail, and so she slinks off to another chair far away. The friends from the twentieth century know not to mention this, especially to me. On some days, when my father couldn't bring himself to visit the center, or when he would call in sick to work, I would know not to ask him why.

Over the course of the funeral, I catch this woman making eye contact with me and I try to make clear that I will not speak with her. But it's so difficult to communicate clearly in mime. My upward-turned eyes, wrinkled forehead, and tightly clenched lips can only convey so much. It can stop her from talking to me, but it can never stop her curiosity, and more often a contorted face makes curiosity even more powerful. Only knowing the truth about my father can end her curiosity, and I am not about to tell her.

This woman is one of the genuinely old elderly people from the seniors' center. When she leans toward my ear to speak her useless condolences, I smell dust and moisturizer. She speaks with the voice of a woman who had grown too old and too accustomed to comforting the younger children of her dead and dying friends. I think I overhear her whispering a prayer for my dad. That woman is too ordinary, too typical to know what obsessed my father for these past fifteen years. If I were to tell her, she'd lie awake at night crying, wishing she had never been so curious. I don't want to do that to her.

The reverend is from the United Church my father used to attend when I was a child. He's a sensible, unremarkable man in middle age—maybe no more than ten years older than I am—going through his funeral motions. We spoke on the phone to plan the funeral, and he knows that no one but him is to say anything. Even these few words are platitudes, clichés. "We remember a loving father, a devoted husband." His few new friends don't know enough about him to say anything worthy of standing in front of a podium. His old friends know enough to keep quiet. I'm certainly not about to say anything of substance today. The purpose of this funeral is to remember someone we all cared about. I don't want to frighten people.

An old woman with faded white hair and glasses sits next to me and I say hello to my father's sister Danielle. She asks if I want to talk. I tell her no. "You're both too stubborn." After fifteen years of stonewalling, she's fed up. So am I, but it's not as if I know how to stop. "You think I didn't try to introduce him to people too, after a while? Obsession isn't good for anyone, under any circumstance. Moths get obsessed, drawn to flames, and they burn up. We're not insects, Marilyn, we're better than insects. We can think, for God's sake." Aunt Danielle is old enough to have earned this kind of bitterness. When I take a few minutes to think about growing old, or the large number of minutes I took to think about it the year I turned thirty, I imagine that collecting a pension gives you permission to stop censoring yourself for public consumption. You can share your feelings of frustration and anger with the world with a freedom that doesn't exist for younger people. You no longer bear annoyances with silence, but can launch whatever tirade strikes you as appropriate, and people will tolerate it because you're old and you're expected to be cranky about what's different from forty years ago. Aunt Danielle is definitely frustrated with dad, not having taken her eyes off his coffin for at least five minutes of telling me what I already know. Hours spent on the phone with officials and secretaries (mostly secretaries) at the Transportation Security Authority. Days and nights locked inside his bedroom teaching himself the forensics of airplane crashes until he finally fell asleep over his textbooks and laptop. Watching him motivated me to finish all my assignments at college with time to spare. I wanted to give myself the kind of life he walked out on, no matter how often Aunt Danielle and I tried to pull him back in. Finally, she runs out of breath, her shoulders relaxing from the tension that held them taut for fifteen years. All she can say now is almost a croak. "He's my little brother."

Aunt Danielle waits alone in her car for the end of the funeral. I'll meet her there as soon as the rest of the crowd leaves and goes home to forget their absent friend Paul, who never really wanted their friendship anymore anyway. I hear a few more stories of dad when he was younger. He and Zoiey once turned a friend's wedding into a dance competition—one hundred dollars to the winning couple—which they won because they were the only people who still cared about the bet by the time the hotel staff kicked everyone out of the reception hall. In his college days, he challenged a group of drunk engineers at a house party next door to a drag race, whose route took them straight past the local police station. After the engineers were written up for DWIs, they never held parties at that house again. He pulled that stunt so he could get some sleep for once on a Thursday night. All the stories I overhear are like this, and I can put dates to all of them. Some are from college, some from his early married years, some when I was a toddler or a baby. Not a single story happened this century. None of the old friends mentioned the last fifteen years. They wouldn't want to know.

The funeral director tells me that everything is prepared and paid for, that they will take care of the cremation and email me when the urn is ready. As he thanks me for choosing their services, I notice someone who arrived late, not so late that everyone was leaving, but late enough to be conspicuous, to make someone wonder if he read the time correctly. He doesn't seem to know anyone else, but keeps looking in my direction. His copper face has an uncertain quality.

When I catch him looking in my direction, his face is smooth, like a man a little younger than me. But as soon as I look into his eyes, he turns away like an embarrassed teenager, and in profile I can see wrinkles along his cheeks and neck, crow's feet under the earpiece of his glasses, and his nose seems bigger, his lips disappearing into a tight frown. There isn't a single gray hair on his head, but rather a pitch-black mane of waves slicked backwards, almost long enough to reach his shoulders. His clothes seem too big for him, his pants baggy on his legs, but his shirt wraps his stomach tightly. He is self-conscious about his appearance, hugging his black leather jacket around him when he feels other people's eyes on him. He is unsure of what to do with his hands. The man lingers now at dad's coffin, staring intensely at it, even though the casket has been closed for a while. I try to step quietly toward the funeral home door. Its position relative to the coffin lets me see the face of this stranger, and will let me make a quick exit if I need it. His face twitches as if he can hear me walking, but he stands motionless at the head of the coffin, the tableau of a man deep in prayer with hands clasped at his chest. Through the thick glasses I can see his eyes darting back and forth beneath his eyelids. They open suddenly as though emerging from a wild dream, his face startled and terrified for a brief instant. Then the stranger is quizzical, as if he only now just recognizes me.

He says something like "excuse me," but it doesn't sound like English. "Would you be Miss Griffith?" I tell him so, and ask his name. "Of course, of course. I am called Pierre. Pierre Masheeno. If you please, forgive me my lateness. It is my first time in Boston, and it took me much time to find this place. I am not familiar wit cities."

"Did you know Paul?" I ask.

He closes his eyes and lowers his head to face the coffin again, but not with the intensity of his earlier expression. Instead, his facial muscles droop into a look of extreme sleepiness. Then he opens his eyes and smiles, exposing graying teeth and concentric circles of wrinkles. I find it impossible to guess his age. "We only met face to face once, in Shawinigan." My heart freezes, and I'm sure I give away my sudden anxiousness. This was a man from dad's trip up north to the crash site. After his time in Canada, his hair had turned white instead of gray, and his skin was ashen, wrinkled, and bruised more easily. Aunt Danielle had to travel to Canada to bring dad back. She never mentioned meeting anyone who looked like this man. "But we talked many times in the last years. Sur la telephone. On the internet. He would ask many, many questions."

I ask why he came here. He exhales deeply, almost too much air for a person to hold in his lungs, before answering in his harsh, gargling accent. "I come here to apologize. I talked to your father a lot. But I told to him too little. ... Do you understand what I mean?"

I have no idea what he means. At least his accent isn't as incomprehensible as I thought it would be when he first spoke. His hands stay motionless on his chest, but his face strains to express what he feels. "I wanted to finally explain. We only know that we must explain everyting de moment we lose the one to who we must talk." He sighs, searching for words in a language that is not his. I can only imagine how difficult it must be for him, but I can feel his nerves. His stress radiates through the room. He swallows a cough, then says, "I have so much to talk. So much to say. I cannot talk here. There is too much to say." He takes a couple of steps toward me, a heavyset man who seems so small, so sad, as if it was *his* father in the casket. I shake the hand he offers me. "Pauls come to Quebec searching for what happened to his wife. I live... My people live... We are Maytee peoples and we live close to where she died. He would come for answers and... he would not find dem. Because in my town, I know de most English, so I would talk to him. All de times Pauls reads about Quebec and comes to Quebec but he never learn a word of my language." The stranger smiles, almost like the old men and women who spent today laughing about when my father was their friend. "You know, it is just a ting we say in Canada about you Americans. You never think to learn a language but your own!"

If he didn't clearly care so much about dad, his laugh would disturb me. In fact, it does anyway with its weird undertone and low-pitched rapid click. "Five year ago, I drive a long way to meet him in Shawinigan, but…" We can both see the funeral director looking at us from the far side of the room, in which we three are the only people left. He gestures for us to leave, that the funeral is over and there is work to be done that we do not need to see. The stranger continues. "We cannot talk now, but dere is so much to say. I stay in Boston until—" He shook his head, trying to remember the word. "No, Wednesday. Please call, and meet me if you can. I ave so much to talk. I can only commontz to explain. No, not commontz." He shakes his head, embarrassed. "Start. I can only start to explain."

He hands me a piece of paper torn from a notepad, a handwritten scrawl that reads:

> Pierre Maschinot
> staying at
> Club Dimes, Boston
> Room 404
> 167 Devonshire Street
> mobile – 819 279 4933

He says goodbye in that strange accent, and I watch him walk through the parking lot. I wonder which of the few cars left is his, but he approaches none of them, instead striding down the sidewalk, his hands stuffed in the pockets of his jacket. I watch until he rounds a corner far in the distance and disappears around a building. Aunt Danielle gets out of the car and asks me what I'm staring after. Now I'm the embarrassed one, saying "Nothing, no one." Pierre's note is still in my hand.

My aunt and I exchange silence as she drives to my building. I go along with her asking to come in for a coffee, even though I just want to be alone. She finally asks me about the piece of paper in my hand, which reminds me to set it on the coffee table. I tell her about Pierre, what he said to me about meeting dad in Canada, talking with him about the crash site. It's difficult to form the words, and even more difficult to make sense of what he told me. I don't mention the ambiguous, shifting quality of his face, the odd way he filled out too much and too little of his clothes, the mysterious colors in his eyes. Aunt Danielle's face beams, her eyes wide with fascination. "Do you think he knows something about what happened to Zoiey?"

"I know what happened to her. She died. Airplanes crash sometimes, and mom was in one of them. That's all. Are you going to drive yourself crazy about it now, too? Dad's not here to go crazy over it anymore…" She stands up and hugs me, starting to cry. She dries the tears on my face, says she's sorry. I don't really know when we stopped crying, but it takes long enough that the coffee is cold once I return to it.

I have heard this question so many times, the question of what really happened to my mother, and no answer I could give would ever be good enough. The only explanation I could ever imagine was that airplanes crash and people die. Every year or two, dad would focus so intensely on his investigations that Aunt Danielle and I would have to stage an intervention of sorts, trying to convince him that there was no mystery to her death. It was an accident, something that happened, a horrible event, but an event like any other. And he would make us relive the first weeks and months after she died. I didn't see it at first, but I should have. People can't see anything past the tips of their own noses when they're seventeen years old. Dad may have lost his wife, but I lost my mother, and it felt so much more important, something he could never understand because he, at least, remembered what a life without mom was like. But I should have seen it, that he never believed that it was just a plane crash no matter how many times we said so. Maybe instead of looking I should have listened, to catch some waver in his voice, some spasm that would tell us that he never really paid attention, never took us seriously when we would just repeat the same old platitudes as the last intervention. "Each time, I thought we got through to him." My aunt's hands shake from stress, the preliminary signs of a disease that I know is going to kill her in five or ten years. Yet even the incremental death Danielle faces whenever she looks at her unsteady hand will come after a decade more of life than her brother experienced.

It's easy to hide an obsession, lay it aside for a while, knowing you'll pick it up again when the attention people pay to you lapses. Attention always lapses in time. If anything is reliable, it's that people can't care about you incessantly, that they will always have concerns that take priority over their concern for you: school, jobs, men. After the grief first subsided, I would dread these relapses of his obsession. I would have to leave my courses, my work, my boyfriends, to help dad find something to think about aside from satellite radar analyses of western Quebec in 1997. And when I returned, the course grades were never as good as they could have been. My managers at work never looked at me with the same sense of reliability as before I left a job to make sure my father would remember to eat. Men would never say why they were irritated with me after I came back. But I knew, and it would burn me when, no matter how hard I tried, I could never find someone who wouldn't feel that jealousy, the repulsive feeling that there's someone in her life more important than them. The walking belly-laugh with his giant arms and sarcastic cackle was gone, and no matter how much I loved that man, he was never coming back. I only saw something wasting away.

Aunt Danielle clasps her hands in front of her mouth, pressing them against her face to keep them steady, but also to suppress the fear in her eyes. "… We never met any of the people he contacted until now. I didn't even believe they were real…." But he met someone in the Quebec backwoods. You don't just drive to cottage country and physically age a decade by getting lost looking for the bar at a ski lodge. "I don't know what you ever thought about what Paul was doing." Danielle always knew what I thought of my father's obsession, and I never would have been any less than resolutely honest with her about it. "Alright, yes, that's correct, I know. I never thought there was anything to discover. I didn't know he was actually talking to people. I mean, there were people who took him seriously." There was at least one: a quiet, haunting man who came all the way from the middle of a Canadian forest to downtown Boston just to make peace with dad, to apologize to him for some unknown injury.

"You know what Pierre said to me?" I ask Aunt Danielle. "He said he's not familiar with cities. He must be about forty years old and he's probably never been to a city before in his life."

"He came all the way here just to say goodbye to Paul?" My eyes can't look away from the crumpled but neatly folded piece of paper sitting on the table. His motel address and phone number. I know that he also came to this noisy forest of concrete—it must be so strange to him, like another planet—not just to make peace with my father's ghost, but to talk to me as well. My aunt doesn't need to know that he came to apologize to me as well as my father. Even if she did need to know, I will never tell her. "Honey, you have to talk to him. Find out what he knows about what happened to your father in Quebec. Maybe he really does know something about—"

Danielle stops here, catching herself short, almost as if she wanted me to finish the sentence, to take on the obsession that propelled my father. But I keep my mouth shut. I refuse to acknowledge that he was driving toward something real, that he tortured himself for a purpose other than his own instability. I refuse to admit that the tangle of wreckage smoldering in a forest was more than an accident. Yet for the first time, I really do consider it. Under the shifting colors of Pierre's dark eyes, there was a sorrow straining to escape. I know that I have to call that number before Wednesday, but I won't call yet.

Pierre's contact information is back in my pocket the moment that Aunt Danielle guides me to the kitchen to rinse the coffee mugs before she drives me to dad's apartment. Before contacting my strange northern guest and perhaps learning the secret story of my father's investigations, I have to prepare. He has files there, charts from his research, and journals of his thoughts and reflections that attempt to make sense of a rudderless world where he could find no direction. He never had to hide his obsession, because in the last few years I would never come into his apartment if I could avoid it. His boxes, books, and charts would send a shiver down my spine when I saw them, closed or open. I knew that if they still existed, then he could relapse at any time, forgetting the world as his entire life became that crash site. For me, they were signs of his growing unhinged. Now I must seriously consider the possibility that he was close to understanding more of that world than I could even notice existed.

Danielle's key turns in the lock, and I step through his door before I become aware enough to turn away from what I'm about to do. Turning away would be rational, and what I am doing here is giving into the madness that I know withered my father. The fear in this space is palpable, thick, exhausting. It's a fear of stepping away from a world where there is no higher order, where sometimes accidents happen for no reason. In this apartment, the world is entirely explicable, ordered, rational, and there is a sinister reason to be uncovered for why my mother is dead in a gouge of twisted metal. I feel the memory of fear, the same as fear itself. It's the combined weight of fifteen years of fear that there is more to understand—fear of a world made of terrifying mysteries that, even more horrific than the questions, *can* be solved. My elderly aunt in the early stages of Parkinson's disease grips my shoulders with her bony hands, and with her touch and voice reassuring me, I can make my legs work again.

She still has to get me a cup of something, or so she says, as she runs into the small kitchen of the apartment and rummages in the cupboards. She prolongs what should be a simple activity by ducking her head back into the main room to ask if I'm alright. I find it irritating how often she asks, but as I can't remember how I got from the entrance of dad's apartment to my seat on the couch, I think her concern is justified. My knees hurt as if they had smacked the hardwood floor, and my head swims with dizziness. Aunt Danielle returns to the sofa with a steaming mug of tea, and I rest it on my thigh while keeping a tight grip on the handle. She asks again if I feel alright, but I ignore her question by asking, "There's still tea here?" It turns out that dad's kitchen cabinet is half full. Even some juice bottles and wilting vegetables still occupy the fridge. I tell Danielle we should pack the non-expired items in the trunk when we leave and bring it to one of the local food banks rather than let it go bad. "We'll have to get the apartment cleaned anyway," she answers. "The landlord will want it occupied soon."

My aunt sits next to me, watching my face closely, probably looking for signs of stress. My vision is better now. It was hard to focus when I first sat on the sofa. Drinking tea does nothing to restore my sense of self-possession, but I sip from the mug a few times to satisfy Aunt Danielle that I am, in fact, perfectly fine to go through dad's files. Even so, the first few times I try to demonstrate that I feel well enough to read them, splashes of tea appear on my pants. The mug is only half full. I wish Aunt Danielle would stop looking at me with that fretting concern in her eyes. She tries to distract me with trivial comments about how to dismantle the apartment over the next few days, but I am finally sick of it and send her to look for his records of the search. If I came here to understand my father's motivations, then I won't put it off because of a dizzy spell.

I wonder how often dad had analyzed, re-analyzed, and re-organized all these papers and records, how long he sat alone in this apartment trying to piece together some coherent narrative of what had happened to his wife. My breathing grows faster, shorter, and my vision starts to lose focus again.

Then Aunt Danielle returns with the first of what would turn out to be several boxes. The collection of documents was organized eccentrically, but its structure becomes clear after a while. Two boxes were designated for what I can best call scientific background material. There are records of weather conditions for the entire flight path my mother's airplane took that day. He collected textbooks and journal articles on aircraft engineering and its basic physics, alongside all the technical forensic reports on the crash itself. I guess he had to make sure he could understand all the science in the reports. Spreading all these papers before me on the apartment floor, what seems most tangential to the scientific papers is a set of documents dad had written himself on the history of the area where the crash happened. Particular attention is paid to a small town called Seul-Coeur. I have no idea how to pronounce it, but when I say "Soul-Coor," it makes Aunt Danielle laugh enough that I know I have it wrong. She says it correctly for me, which sounds more like "Saul-Caar."

"Literally, it means One-Heart or Only-Heart," she tells me. "It really is in the middle of nowhere, isn't it?" Dad has several maps of the area in the scientific boxes, which lets me figure out precisely where this collection of houses actually is. As far as I can tell, it's hidden in the nooks and crannies of lakes and rivers deep inside Quebec. On some of these maps, there isn't even a road leading to where this town should be, which I didn't think was possible anymore in North America. Because there are so few historical records that make reference to the area, the origin of the town is at best hazy. It's a region so inconsequential and devoid of interest that even calling it mundane would be a compliment. Seul-Coeur was indistinguishable from most of the country's interior, an utterly unremarkable village until a plane crashed there in 1997. Even then, it seemed to be utterly unremarkable to everyone except Paul Griffith. No one really lived in the area before the early 1800s. Even the Cree largely stayed away or just passed through without giving the place much thought. But by the beginning of the twentieth century, it was part of a disparate collection of villages and towns that formed a fairly bustling, if unexceptional, network of trade in the area, inhabited by Mettiss people.

Aunt Danielle laughs at me again, and corrects my pronunciation. "They're called Métis, dear!" Irritated with her corrections, I order her back to the kitchen to make something for us to eat while I continue exploring the boxes. I remember that word was how Pierre described the people of his town, which dad in his file says are descended from mixed Native and French settler families that constitute a sizable minority of the Native population of this part of Canada. I'm fixed on this word, Métis, wondering how that combination of letters could be associated with those sounds, and how my aunt's grade school exposure to French fifty years ago still leaves her better equipped than I am to read these words.

I move on to the other boxes dedicated to material directly relating to the crash: copies of TSA documents analyzing the plane and black box, police reports from American and Canadian authorities, and, where dad couldn't find copies of the actual reports, transcripts of interviews with the police officers who wrote them. Most illuminating will be dad's own notebooks, his leather-bound journals that are his personal writings on the crash, the official investigation, and his own investigation. I can't open these yet.

Aunt Danielle joins me on the floor of the living room and clears a space in the sprawl of papers and documents to set down two plates of cheap pasta, spoons, and forks. We eat while sorting through official reports of the crash, along with dad's notes and journals analyzing the analyses. We search for inconsistencies and the inexplicable. I find a lot that's inexplicable in these reports, considering that their primary purpose is to explain what had happened. The first elements of weirdness to appear didn't even seem very strange at first. Every report from a Canadian or American transport safety or police authority described how difficult it was to get to the crash site. Initially, I considered this a mundane detail explaining the thickness of the woods, the winding paths between the lakes and rivers. But this "difficulty of access" detail surfaced in several other reports of the crash investigation, habitual complaints even of simply trying to get to Seul-Coeur from the region's major urban center, a town called Rouyn-Noranda. I'm not about to try to pronounce it. It speaks to the smallness of such a vast region that what I described as a major urban center apparently has a population of 40,000. Even local police officers, people who had lived in the area their entire lives, had trouble finding Seul-Coeur. They would drive in different directions, east for a few miles, then west for a few more. Some locals in Rouyn-Noranda even said it wasn't worth going near Seul-Coeur itself, that the town could never supply answers to questions. But this crabbiness sounds more like typical rural town rivalries that generate rumors of inbreeding and unaccountable birth defects, similar nonsense to what people often said about "hillbilly country" in the South.

Dad sometimes managed to interview some officials more than once, and the later transcripts are often more revealing than the earlier ones, as people are less obligated to maintain confidentiality on long-inactive cases. The Canadian investigators all came from that region of western Quebec, were familiar with the area, the town of Rouyn-Noranda, and the surrounding villages and communities. The American investigators knew almost nothing about this part of Quebec, often relying on locals to translate written documents and verbal testimony into English. Most of the locals didn't know enough English for the task, if they knew any English at all. Two Americans my father interviewed in 2005 were peculiarly suspicious of their French-speaking counterparts and assistants. Both were certain that there were many details of the incident about which they were never told. They would see town police, sheriffs, and officials from the mayor's office all talking very seriously in hushed French. They were certain these secret conversations were about the crash through overhearing particular French words they had picked up, or that were similar enough to English that they could guess. But the few times they could get reasonable translators, even then they received only a couple of sentences summarizing a conversation among French speakers that had lasted ten minutes. Their suspicions never went in the official reports, because they were based only on circumstantial evidence, and they were under orders from their superiors not to record anything in official documents that would complicate the relationship between

Canada and the State Department on matters of air traffic security. This pressure became especially fierce after 2001, of course, when American files were transferred to the Department of Homeland Security. But a couple of years after that, the people my father interviewed had retired or no longer worked with the government. So they could speak their minds fully. I also bear in mind that dad's interview subjects could be growing less reliable as the years pass, their memories embellishing, supplementing, or misconstruing the events as they happened. The haze of memory tends to justify paranoia.

I think I've finally become accustomed to the walls of this apartment, as if focusing on the puzzle of the disappearance is adjusting me to its shape. It's good that I'm more comfortable here as the sun sets, because the documents I'm reading now are strange enough to unnerve me on their own. Aunt Danielle is lying on the sofa, pretending that she is only resting her eyes when I know she's napping. I don't think she would want to read this document, though, a TSA transcript of the plane's black box recording of the cockpit conversations. I skip ahead to the moment the airplane flies over western Quebec, as it approaches the place where it would become a field of twisted, smoking debris. There are breaks in the transcript as the writer tries to describe some of the background noises, which he says he has never heard in a black box recording. He describes a kind of rapid, polyrhythmic clicking, like scraping the fingernails of a jittering hand across granite. There are distortions in the dialogue, long stretches of the recording where the conversation is still taking place using some kind of language that might be English. The transcriber says he can make sense of some words, but that he doesn't trust his ears to decipher this section of the tape, which sounds not unlike voices in reverse, but the recording apparently lacks the warping sound of being played backwards. Instead, he writes that the tape sounds as if it is running sideways. I laugh when I see that my dad has annotated this section with a huge "WTF!?" scrawled in red marker. I'm glad that he never lost his sense of humor completely.

I scrub a tear out of my eye with a finger and begin reading through a report on the crash site itself, particularly the attempt to reconstruct the aircraft from the collection of wreckage. It surprises me to learn that this wholesale reconstruction of a crashed airplane from its recovered debris is a standard forensic procedure. It makes for a giant, three-dimensional, almost necessarily incomplete and macabre jigsaw puzzle. Yet even when the crash takes place over a small area on land, not every piece is recovered for the reconstruction. Maybe some pieces of the aircraft are too badly damaged or burned, bent out of their shape, or have just plain disintegrated. My mother's flight seems to have suffered the opposite problem. The investigators found numerous pieces of wreckage that clearly came from the aircraft. Some of it was even marked with company logos. But they had already discovered this part of the plane, pounded into a different shape and thrown in a different direction on impact. It was as if the metal had cloned itself. Investigators counted at least eight different pieces of wreckage, each no bigger than a person's chest, which had at least one almost-duplicate. According to dad's files, there may have been thirty pieces of duplicated wreckage, but different members of the investigative team couldn't agree on identifying each piece. The effort to reconstruct the aircraft stalled thanks to these disagreements, then was abandoned entirely within a year.

The files on the wreckage were strange to say the least. But what really held my attention was what the police, investigators, and my father thought of the townspeople. Just as I open the first of these files, Aunt Danielle, too tired to drive her own car, asks me to take her home. Only now do I realize that the sun has long set, and that I've been here for hours, poring over these documents with a single-mindedness that unnerves me, reminding me of the moods that used to terrify me when I saw them in my father. He would be alone in his apartment, hunched over books and reports, unshaven for weeks, always grumbling and sometimes howling. He allowed no one to rouse him back into the world.

I collect the notebooks and files that I haven't yet read, as well as dad's private journals, and load them into the back seat of Aunt Danielle's car. I ask her if she minds my staying at her house tonight. "Of course, dear. If you don't mind sleeping on that lumpy futon." I don't find her futon that lumpy, and I need to know that someone is with me tonight. I may not say a word to her from the moment I shut the door of her storage room with that decrepit blue futon until the next morning, but I simply need the sensation of another life around me. She turns out all the lights in her house except in the room where I'll sleep, with the last of my father's files and journals piled in a stack on the floor next to me. My eyes are tired, sunken in their sockets, and straining to focus in the washed-out orange light of the room's only lamp. But I have to read.

The forensic investigators say nothing about the people of Seul-Coeur, but the police have a few scattered observations. Dad has photocopied the few pages from police reports that mention the locals, and collected them in this single file along with transcripts of his discussions with Pierre. All the people the police speak to are cagey, evasive, always insisting that they saw nothing of the wreck. They sometimes said they heard the sound of a plane in the distance, but can never say when. Those who do give times, even just rounded to the nearest hour, never agree with each other, and never agree with the aircraft's own black box. Refusals of local people to give witness accounts are usually laced with contempt for the police, and for outsiders in general. It sounds typical of isolated country people to me, folks who don't appreciate the presence of strange faces who ask strange questions. But one police report devotes some detail to describing a man named Louis Rechappagedunord. I stare at this surname on the page for a moment, unable to imagine how to say it. Then I keep reading. The officer is highly disturbed by a tendency for the man to focus his eyes as if he is looking through him while they talk. Most of the time when someone's eyes are unfocused this way, it's a sign of indifference, or boredom, or contempt. But Louis stared through this police officer with such intense concentration that it felt as if the man were staring not at his skin, but at his skeleton. The officer felt a bizarre, unseasonal static electricity in the air when speaking to Louis, and his heartbeat quickened more than only nervousness could excuse.

As I open my father's interview transcript, I wonder if this is the same way Pierre spoke with him. Pierre's words on the transcript read with the same humble tone he took with me this afternoon. When he spoke to me, he wanted to talk, and his failure to explain fully what he wanted was an effect of his nerves and what little time we had at the funeral home. I could tell that he wanted so badly to admit something to me. Yet in this transcript, his goal is to safeguard what he knows, to reveal nothing to my father. Pierre dances around questions, laughs his way through serious inquiries, denies knowledge of what my father's investigation has convinced him he must at least be slightly familiar with. No matter how hard he tries to get any information from him whatsoever, Pierre in this conversation will not even betray a hint. Dad's journal still waits for me, unopened. Out of all the material that he has assembled over all these years, I must deal with this last. I am too tired by now to begin reading it. I somehow find the energy to reach my hand up to the lamp's switch and turn it off, then fall back on the futon. My body feels encrusted with the thickness of fatigue, and I'm asleep immediately.

I sleep almost too well, and I'm sure when I wake up in the morning that I had terrible dreams of which I remember nothing. I take a shower and put on yesterday's clothes, the same black skirt and blouse from my father's funeral. I carry his journal downstairs with me to the kitchen, where I make coffee, and can hear Aunt Danielle creeping to the bathroom upstairs. I leave the pot turned on for when she comes downstairs, and step outside to sit on the porch alone, to watch a neighborhood buzzing in its morning routine of a bright early summer. I feel myself growing more alert with the influence of the coffee and sunlight. I rub my fingers along the spine of my father's leather journal, fixed on a single question among the hundreds that would naturally arise from those files, one mystery among all that has yet to be explained. I cannot reconcile the contrite, profoundly sad man I met yesterday with the man in that interview transcript who delighted in misdirecting and confusing my father. Unlike all the technical forensic questions and inexplicable anomalies of my father's files, this one is easy to answer. I take my phone out of my pocket. If this question is so easy, I wonder why my heart is beating so rapidly as I gaze at the piece of paper where Pierre has written his Boston address until Wednesday. I wonder why it takes me so long to push those buttons on the slick touchscreen. I pause and brush my fingers along glass that glows with cold, steady light, hoping that someone will call me, that I'll never have to finish dialing. After a moment, there are two rings.

"Bonjour Allo!" I hear.

2

I have to spend Monday dealing with the final residues of my father, particularly getting his furniture moved out so that his landlord can put the apartment on the market. The moving company was already arranged, but they need supervision because Aunt Danielle is paranoid about movers stealing things. So I drive home to change into more comfortable clothes, and spend all day outside dad's apartment watching the movers stick his furniture in their truck and drive it to the storage unit where it will be photographed, thrown on Craigslist, and rescued by anyone comfortable with owning a dead man's mediocre IKEA legacy. Danielle agreed to take care of handling potential buyers over email and the phone, and even though she insists I take all the money from the sales, I convince her to split it with me. I have to spend Tuesday arguing with my boss for extended time off from work to deal with my father's estate and the unexpected need for me to go to Quebec for a week or more. Of course, I tell him nothing about my father's search, or Pierre and the phone conversation we had in the early hours of Monday morning when I realized I would have to go with him to Quebec. Mr. Casullo is irritated, but by the end of the day, he doesn't mind. He even asks if he can be of any help sorting through the details of (as I've told him) my father's property holdings in rural Canada that he had kept secret from me. Property management is what we do for a living here, but I tell him it shouldn't be necessary, and that I can handle the details myself. We arrange for Tom to handle any of my clients that visit the office while I'm away, and I settle the last details of my work before I meet Pierre.

We've arranged to discuss the trip to Quebec in more detail at a Vietnamese restaurant located in the neighborhood of Pierre's hotel. Because of his ignorance of Boston and cities more generally, he asked me to choose where we should meet. I wasn't sure if he would be comfortable in a Vietnamese place. "Nonsense. Because I know nothing about it is why I want to go." I've never heard anyone get excited by a description of phổ, the spicy beef soup that I suppose is the Vietnamese equivalent of truck-stop food, and this only adds to the ways this strange man continues to intrigue me. I'm running late after taking longer at work than I anticipated when I first made the reservation, but I expect correctly that Pierre will get lost on the way there.

When he finally arrives I wave to him as he stands talking to the hostess. He seems not to be aware that most restaurants have a hostess that seats you at a particular place, that you aren't always free just to walk inside wherever you want. Nonetheless, as soon as he sees me wave, he bounds toward me without even a glance back at the annoyed hostess and sits down with me. I have forgotten until now how much Pierre's physiology, the way he carried himself, disturbed me at the funeral, but watching his loping gait reignites that feeling of unease. He removes his sunglasses and blinks too many times, far more frequently than anyone would feel necessary, as if trying to make his vision of the world resemble a strobe light. "De sun has been too bright today." I ask if the brightness makes him feel uncomfortable, and his head jerks up to look at me, his face betraying a glimpse of fright, as if I have stumbled onto some information, some facet of his biology that he doesn't want known. But he quickly returns to the jovial mood I remember from the end of our phone conversation yesterday, picking up the menu and staring dazzled at the pictures of pork balls and beef intestine.

"There is so much to see here in Boston, to experience, to sense." I've never heard the word "sense" used that way, in such an ordinary, non-academic voice, talking about sensation. I ask him what he means by that. "Everything moves in so many directions, sometimes so many directions at once. These are not the kinds of things I am used to seeing move dis way." Pierre studies the menu like an adolescent boy seeing naked breasts for the first time, and it doesn't take me long to realize that this is probably the first time he has ever been inside a Vietnamese restaurant, eaten Asian food, or even seen this ethnicity of people. A man who is unfamiliar with cities is a man I don't think I can understand. "I have never seen streets filled with cars so thick dey can't even move anymore. And dey honk all de time. How do you ever stand dis noise of honking?" I explain simply that I grew up here, that a city is filled with people constantly on their way somewhere, with demands on their time. I've always pictured life in small towns, which I suppose is life in Seul-Coeur, as quiet, peaceful to the point of boredom. "Seul-Coeur is certainly quiet." I ask Pierre to tell me more about his experiences here over the past few days, and he tells story after story of how baffled he was trying to find his way around the airport, or the strangeness of our elevated highways and bridges. He's ridden the subway a few times, which he says is extremely comfortable to him. He spent all yesterday riding the different routes of our subway system, exploring all their corners, even in the neighborhoods where most people don't like to go anymore.

This man who can be no younger than forty speaks with the giddy enthusiasm of a child. Someone at his age isn't supposed to have retained any sense of wonder. As I grew accustomed to his accent and his eccentric choice of words, I was beginning to understand him more consistently. His grin appears to stretch far too wide over his face as he speaks of exploring my strange land called Boston, his eyes darting too fast over the pages of the menu, staring engrossed at one image, then zigzagging faster than I could follow. When we finish dinner, his gait from the table to the entrance is almost a gallop, as if he expects to have more than two legs. Each time I look back at his face, his wrinkles seem to have shifted—not only their depth and number, but somehow their arrangement. Do I really trust this man enough to let him take me to this town whose infamy was so incredible to me?

✳ ✳ ✳

At last, I have found someone in Seul-Coeur who will answer my questions, or at least take them seriously enough to consider answering. My journal can now be something other than a chronicle of failure, mystery, and disappointment. I suppose there can at least be some hope. Literally years of attempts to correspond with officials in the city government or the local police have been stonewalled each time. Do they think rude and threatening refusals to talk actually discourage people from investigating that dank town? It only fascinates them more. I reviewed the latest satellite imagery of the area and found more of the same: woods, shops, houses, woods, a few small vegetable plots, more woods, the lake, and woods. Only a place as sinister as Seul-Coeur could look so normal. There's something sinister in a town whose people would be so hostile to a man only trying to find out what happened to his wife.

This sign of progress comes with a puzzling new discovery. As part of their duties of monitoring the airspace over North America for nuclear attack, NORAD kept watch over the years for any strange energies in the continent whatsoever, any sign of Soviet technological infiltration. It was an era of suspicion and desperation, haunted by the fear that another superweapon might be around the corner. Stalemate is a tension that can break a man. Things are supposed to survive by change and adaptation. But in a stalemate, survival is a function of silence, immovability, making yourself as impassable as a mountain, a single force more powerful than any who try to stop you. You must become unshakeable.

My collection of evidence related to Zoiey's case now includes copies of the government charts recording all data on the energy fields. The Cold War having been finished for so long, the government could decide with a clear conscience to release, or at least loosen their grip on, any data deemed unimportant to national security or otherwise anomalous. More afraid of terrorists with briefcase bombs than bureaucrats with missile launch codes, information about mysterious fluctuations in magnetic fields could be given to ecologists, geophysicists, and anyone else who aspires to be an amateur crackpot. I know where I fit in these categories.

The NORAD data describes a series of fluctuations in the magnetic field of the planet, the epicenter of which are always around Lac du Monarque, Quebec. These fluctuations appear at regular intervals, every seven years, four months, and sixteen days. They grow in intensity for six days, climaxing in a kind of magnetic explosion. It isn't an electromagnetic pulse of the kind that is constructed to fry computer machinery. There is simply a pattern in the field, a complicated arrangement that is not quite complicated enough to have arisen naturally. It begins in the magnetic field over Seul-Coeur and Lac du Monarque, spreads outward over western Quebec, propagates into the ionosphere, and finally leaves the magnetic field of Earth through its most distant reaches. The whole process takes about three months. Its effects in the meantime are not catastrophic on large scales. It seems to cause blackouts in local power grids, airplane navigational systems to become confused, and compasses to go a little haywire in some places near the origin of the pattern. But the energy pulse before the most recent one coincided perfectly with Zoiey's plane going down. I can only surmise that, while flying through the region affected by the change in magnetic activity, the plane's equipment became confused to the point of catastrophe.

But I have also compared the NORAD data on the magnetic field distortions with TSA records of plane crashes in the area the field affects. That data was always public. There is no correlation between the two, no spikes in plane crashes in that region at the times when the pattern develops and spreads. There is something this data is hiding from me, something for which I will finally need to infiltrate Seul-Coeur, to discover the secret behind the electromagnetic disturbance. It is almost time for the pattern to appear over the region again, an event that, if I can witness it, may finally reveal the mystery of Seul-Coeur to me. In all my previous trips to the region, something has always prevented me from reaching Lac du Monarque. I have always been stuck in a ski resort town or cottage country, close enough for people to know what town I was talking about, but still removed enough from the region that no one I spoke with knew any facts or would tell me anything noteworthy. But now I have the possibility of a man on the inside, someone trusted by the town government, but who may be willing to reveal some of its secrets. First, I am to meet him in Shawinigan, the resort town where I usually get stuck trying to reach Seul-Coeur. Although he has not promised me that we will go to Seul-Coeur, he was the first to broach the possibility of a visit with me, which no other resident of that crepuscular town has ever done. This man Maschinot may be the first sympathetic ear I have had offered to me in a long time.

* * *

Pierre meets me at my house, and we take a taxi to the airport together from there. He carries his belongings in a brown duffel bag, which he easily fits into the trunk over my black rolling suitcase. The contrast between us is almost funny. When I travel, it's from city to city, often landing in labyrinthine airports so sprawling that I have to navigate them in buses and underground trains. When he travels, it's to campsites, cabins, and fishing holes. Pierre tells me about a week he once spent ice fishing at a lake near the northeastern shore of Hudson Bay, all by himself with nothing but an extra set of winter clothes, a hand drill to puncture the ice, his fishing gear, and a rifle for defense against bears. "You had to defend yourself against bears?" Sometimes a polar bear would slip down from the tundra to that latitude, far more south than what he says is their usual home. He knows there is less ice in the Arctic Ocean than there used to be, so the bears come farther south and farther inland to feed every year. Very few of his people in Seul-Coeur pay attention to those sorts of problems, and although I don't say so, I know it's a typical habit of country people. So I can understand why no one in Seul-Coeur would be interested in helping my father. An outsider could have no influence with people who are that insular. I could tell Pierre was a bit different in that regard.

"Bears, they are precious. To have to kill one is a terrible thing. If you look in their eyes, you can see something like a soul. It is a soul that seriously considers eating you, that's why you need a gun. But it is still a soul. Very rare are people who can see that in a bear."

When we climb out of the taxi, I lead him through the airport to the lineups to check in for international flights. He forgets which pocket he put his passport in, has to be reminded what the maximum size for a carry-on bag is, and doesn't even notice how irritated the girl at the desk is growing as he asks her for the third time to explain, step by excruciating step, how his bag will travel from his hand to the airplane to the baggage counter at the Montreal airport. I was already surprised that he managed to find his way around Boston. Now I'm amazed that he even made it through the airports without being arrested. I lead him past a long line of scowling passengers waiting to check their luggage, who stare at us as if I'm escorting someone from another planet.

I'm wearing ballet flats and no belt, my jacket is in my checked bag, my laptop is out of my carry-on while I'm still waiting in line, so I'm through the security screeners in no time. Pierre crouches down to unlace his hiking boots, meticulously undoing each lace, which holds up the security line behind me for ten minutes. He wears a belt with a heavy stylized oval buckle—which he should have known was bound to set off the metal detectors—and when the officer with the wand orders him to take it off, he hangs it around his neck before being told to put it in a tray to go through the scanner. He asks, "What do you think I hide inside my belt?" which convinces me that his sarcasm is going to get him sent to an interrogation room. Amazingly, they wave him through. I suppose airport security has learned the harmlessness of stupidity.

I chide him for being such an idiot when he's finally through the gauntlet, having earned the combined wrath of everyone on the security staff and in the line behind him. I tell him that if he behaves in every lineup the way he does in this airport, he must not have any friends left. But Pierre is so unfamiliar with airports, he still doesn't know what to expect. "You have been through airports and on planes all your life. Me, I am only here once before when I came last week. … I do not like their scanning machines, not at all." By now, he has only just finished re-lacing one boot. "To be honest, I was happy that the full-body scanners I read about have been taken away. They would give off strange fields, I think. Is field the right word in English?" I have no idea what he's talking about, and he and I both put our misunderstanding down to a difference in language, as I have no clue what the term "field" refers to in French. He says it's of no concern, so I don't press him on the subject, and leave to buy coffee while he finishes lacing his right boot.

We walk to the gate with my coffee and his tea. Pierre seems to shrink from many of the people we encounter in the concourse, made in all shapes, colors, and sizes of humanity. I wonder how many people he interacts with who come from outside Seul-Coeur. From the notes my father left in his journal, it can't be very many, even though he has enough experience with outsiders to have learned English, and he met with dad in Shawinigan. Even so, he said just after he checked in his duffel bag that he had never gotten a passport before he decided that he'd visit Boston. "People in my town don't get too interested in other kinds of people. You know, I came across an expression in English a time ago. I don't know if they use it much anymore. It is the lonely heart." The phrase is old-fashioned, but I know what it means. Pierre laughs, that odd clicking undertone slipping out of the corners of his upward-curling mouth. "Yes, you know Seul-Coeur means in English Only-Heart, as if the people there are not just alone, but they don't want to be anything but alone. It is coincidence. Yet it is very true of my town."

As we wait at the gate for boarding, I realize precisely the amount of time it usually takes to get a passport, so I ask Pierre how long he had planned to come to Boston, and if he intended to speak to my father again before discovering he was dead. His eyes widen, and his hair, usually slicked back, falls a little out of place and perks up, as if his scalp was embarrassed. He speaks haltingly, unsure of what to say first. "You know dat I met your father in Quebec before. Once before." Of course I know. Pierre mentioned it at the funeral, and I have been slowly reading my father's journal. "When I talked to him, I wanted to make sure he stayed away of my town. For a long time, I am like many other people in my town. I did not mind going to the outside, but I did not want outsiders come to Seul-Coeur." Pierre started to relax, although he still couldn't look me in my face while he said this. I had caught him out, and he was clearly uncomfortable. I wouldn't want to lay a confession like this on a person I was about to spend two hours sitting next to on a cramped plane, even if I had promised him the window seat. Yet a weight seems to roll off of him as he speaks. "Pauls wanted to see Seul-Coeur, explore it. He was convinced there were secrets to be found. I wanted him to go home and give up. He was not that old and ad much time left. Our town was nothing to be obsessed wit. I was too like the rest of Seul-Coeur. I wished he would leave us alone." He takes a long pause, as if waiting for me to speak, but I have nothing to say. Rather, I have too much to say, and so say nothing. "But he was determined," Pierre continues. "Pauls was very strong-minded. Now I respect that determination more than I respect my town's wanting to be left alone. That is why I wanted to come."

Our seats are called to board, and after Pierre verifies with me that we can, in fact, board the aircraft, he is visibly and audibly relieved to have been interrupted. When we're in line, however, I still have to remind him to be ready to show his passport. We file down the aisle, and I'm glad he's at least managed to work out how the seats are arranged, though he does check the letters on both sides of the plane all the way down until we reach row nine. When the plane rapidly accelerates for takeoff, Pierre's eyes widen with what I have trouble believing is fright, the muscles of his face tensing in an inhuman pattern of sinewy fibers underneath his skin. "I am a little afraid of big planes," he tells me after we reach cruising altitude. "It is so strange for me to have my legs no more rest on earth. A plane in the sky is so visible, so… can be in danger?" I could tell he was searching for an English word in his memory, and I offered him "vulnerable." "Yes… That's the word… Vulnerable."

He spends the journey from Boston to Montreal gazing out the window, entranced by the shapes of the clouds. He tells me that before flying to visit me, he had never seen the top of a cloud, only ever having flown in small, low-altitude planes. It was an ordinary sight to me. He is appalled as I tell him that I've slept through every airplane flight I've taken since I was a little girl. As he gapes out the window, I am disturbed again by his eyes, opening almost too wide, as if he didn't need to blink.

Appalled. Disturbed. Mystified. Did Pierre come here trying to understand me? To understand my father? The search makes detectives of us all. I'm not the only person in the world to lose her mother in a plane crash. Reminding myself of that fact helped me get through losing her fifteen years ago. Dad wasn't the only person in the world to lose his wife in a plane crash either, but the fact never sunk in for him. No, that isn't quite true. My father was never so stupid as to think that no one had dealt with a trauma like his before. The problem was that the pain of all those people was not enough like his for him to find solace in it. In the early years he tried therapy sessions with other people who had lost spouses and family members, after Aunt Danielle and I dragged him there. When we would take him, he would be depressed, but when he came home he was depressed and angry. The others at group therapy had all lost people they loved, but they had lost Michael and Jennifer and Ariel and little Charlie. None of them had lost Zoiey. I couldn't listen to him anymore once he started listing all those names of the dead he cared nothing about. He would only drag me deeper into his pit.

Yet here I am flying into his pit, my guide a man *from* that pit, who emerged from the depths to reconnect with my father. Now he talks to me. I can see the ghosts of his eyes reflected on the inner rim of his glasses if I sit at the proper angle. He has no idea that I'm trying to see his eyes when they are not looking at me, when he isn't trying to control them. I am unnerved by the strange shapes I sense underneath his skin, which is how I've tried to articulate to myself exactly what disturbed me about Pierre when I first saw him, the odd way his clothes hung on his body, as if he could just barely fit into ordinary human shapes. That he could pass for an ordinary person seems more of a coincidence, even though the normality of most people is barely worth remarking on. That's what normality is. A smooth, continuous motion, no bumps or jostling, so relaxed that you barely need notice its movement at all. It's a plane calmly flying through the still air of a cloudless sky, all its parts fitting perfectly together in all their processes and relationships. I hate airplanes. Spending hours stuck in a cramped seat with nothing to do but think. And Pierre is lost in the clouds.

When we land at Montreal airport, Pierre asks a security guard a question in French and gets an extremely long answer. I understand none of the words, but there are a lot of hand gestures involved, and I can guess that Pierre is getting directions. The security guard seems incredulous that Pierre and I, or anyone, would go to that part of the airport. At one point, Pierre says something that makes them both laugh, and I gather this is going to take a while. So I browse through the magazine racks in one of those little newsstand/bookstores that you only find in airports. I recognize most of the people on the covers, the actors and the models. But their names are the only words in these magazines I understand. The political magazines and newspapers are even more cryptic because I'm American and don't know who these politicians are. I think of asking Pierre, but he would likely know nothing about them either because, as far as Seul-Coeur is concerned, they are all outsiders.

He taps me on the shoulder and says we must go to meet the plane that will take us to Rouyn-Noranda. Apparently, we have to cross from one side of the airport to the other. Spending ten minutes getting directions from a security guard, I'd think Pierre had worked out the most direct route, but he still leads me down wide hallways and concourses, under signs in a language that I don't understand. Only the numbers make sense to me, and eventually our route zigzags through so much of the terminal that the order in which I see the numbers on gates and on signs leading to gates lose even that minimal coherence. I'm lost and I can only be led. Pierre's stride seems longer than a person's should, as if his legs came a little disconnected from his hips. I lag behind, wondering if we really have gotten lost despite Pierre's newfound certainty. He hollers at me to catch up, sometimes slipping into outbursts of French. "Marilyn! Allownzee!" I haven't seen this confidence in him before, as if returning to where he feels at home emboldens his step. Pierre no longer needs a guide through a complex, confusing city full of excesses and ethnicities. Now he's the guide and I'm the lost foreigner drifting among incomprehensible words and noises. If I do lose him, I don't know if I'll be able to find my way home again, let alone to Seul-Coeur, so I refuse to slip out of his sight or dally at distractions.

As we near our destination, the crowds thin, and the space between gates grows greater. Eventually we turn a corner that didn't look like anything but a blank wall from down the corridor, descend a wide set of metal steps, and reach a large steel door. Pierre has to heave himself against it to open it, and I worry that security officers will find us. Pierre tells me that this part of the airport is always left alone, but that makes no sense. No part of any airport is left alone anymore. Terrorists could sneak in. "We are no terrorists," he answers, and I'm not sure if he misunderstood my objection, or if he simply doesn't care that he's forced open a secure metal door at an airport, and is leading me on foot across tarmac to a gunmetal gray hangar so dilapidated that parts of it are rusting. Pierre takes me to a side entrance and knocks rapidly four times.

After a moment that lasts just a little too long, a young man with spiky hair wearing a sleeveless white shirt opens the door barely wide enough for him to stand in the gap. His mustache is ridiculous, as if someone had flecked dust irregularly across his upper lip. Despite his unthreatening pubescent appearance, I feel my heartbeat accelerate as he stares at me. He and Pierre are talking in French, but he has fixed me with a glare of unsurpassable hostility. The boy's voice expresses rage without violence, more intimidating to me precisely because he doesn't scream or lose control of himself. Pierre reacts sternly, speaking first calmly, as if he were only relating ordinary facts about the weather or trivial events of the day. Then, as the boy's tone refuses to change, Pierre is sharp, curt, his voice coming more from his gut than his throat. He finally lets one sentence fly out like the bark of a pit bull. I know nothing of what it means, but the boy snaps his eyes away from me. He lets one brief moment of fear cross his eyes as he looks at Pierre, then disappears inside, throwing the door open so hard that it slams back against the metal wall, making the whole hangar resound with a hollow clang.

Pierre catches the door so it doesn't bounce back from the metal wall and lock us out again. He leads me inside and meanders in the hangar. He whispers apologies in my ear on behalf of the boy, his English a little more confused than it was earlier today. I see the boy striding toward a small office in the rear of the hangar, and his legs seem to share the same disconnected quality that I saw in Pierre as he led me through the airport. He does not look back at us, so I try to put him out of my thoughts and let my vision wander over the rest of the hangar, which is nowhere near as cavernous as I expected an airplane hangar to be. I feel as if the curved ceiling bears down on me from above, like the dense cover of black, low-lying rainclouds over the airport that have yet to break. Then I see the airplane that will take us across Quebec. It's a small twin-engine propeller plane, painted the bright blue of a cloudless sky—to camouflage it in flight, I wonder? I think it's a Cessna, but just because that's the only brand name of small aircraft that I know. I hear something like a truck pull away from the front of the hangar, and when I look out through a window, I see mine and Pierre's bags dumped haphazardly on the pavement. An empty baggage handler's flatbed drives off as fast as it can. Pierre appears from behind me to take the bags on the plane.

As he walks me back to the center of the hangar he tells me that, because our bags are here, we can get ready for takeoff. He asks if I need to go to the bathroom before we leave, but I decline. Right now I can see the boy from the hangar's entrance still staring at me with anger as he runs through safety checks at the front of the plane. With him is another underdressed boy with upward-standing hair, who I can tell has at least enough sense to keep himself clean-shaven. They walk with a confident swagger, and their arms and legs move with a disconnected swinging motion suggesting an internal arrangement of their bodies that differs just enough from humanity to make me wonder just who and what they are, if not country bumpkins from an isolated village. Human movements have a kind of casual authenticity, as if the daily tasks of their lives require no effort. These boys are trying too hard. Every few moments, one or both of them will look at me with such gripping intensity that I have to keep myself from clinging to Pierre.

"These aren't the pilots, are they?" I ask, and Pierre confirms that they are. "Rissharr and Jean-Claude have been flying small planes around Quebec since they were fourteen." I see one of them, though I can't tell which one from this far away, stand motionless by the airplane entrance while staring with a blank face at Pierre. "We are ready for you to enter the plane," a boy calls with blunted intonation. When we reach the front of the airplane, the door has been opened and a small wheeled staircase rolled underneath it. The boys have gone inside, presumably to take their places in the cockpit.

Although I can barely stand up straight in this airplane, I'm relieved that the cockpit door is shut and I don't have to look at my adolescent pilots. I need only sit back in my chair and wonder whether they're old enough to understand the instructions manual. I ask Pierre how long it will take to get to Seul-Coeur from here. "Well, we will land in Rouyn-Noranda. Seul-Coeur has no paved airport. De only planes dat come to de town itself are de kinds dat land on water. Dey land on Lac du Monarque at de key. Sorry, I mean quay." I notice that his accent is thicker than it was before we came to the hangar, and he looks agitated, the hair on his arms and the sides of his head seemingly electrified. So I ask if he feels all right, but he promises me, perhaps a little too emphatically, that nothing is wrong. "Me, I am not so good at switching languages. I am no Montréalay." But his words come out too quickly. Something is still gnawing at him, something that boy pilot said to him earlier. Pierre sits quietly, his eyes shut too tightly. If they were open, they would stare directly at the cockpit door. The skin of his face is pulled taut, his mouth a thin line of stress, the same twisted expression he wore while looking at my father's coffin, as if he could see through the wood. I have to turn away from him and face the window, watching the sky as we sail through it, the jackhammering buzz of the propellers keeping me from sleep.

By counting the clouds to hypnotize myself into something like rest, I manage a reverie that is punctuated with the vibrating of the propellers. The rumbling grows heavier, the plane diving up and dipping down with turbulence. The whole plane is jittering, creaking, snapping like a whip. We pitch up and acceleration pushes me into my seat. Then within seconds we pitch back down at such an angle it feels like a nosedive. I can taste stomach acid burning my throat as I imagine us plummeting to earth. The plane pitches upward again as if we were flying directly at the sun. I close my eyes and see myself tumbling end over end, then charred and flattened on the fields and rocks—the past about to repeat itself. This kind of attitude will only cause paralysis. I won't let dad's instability infect me.

The clouds around us grow dark, but not dark like rainclouds. They have no silhouettes of light, even though I know the sun is still shining somewhere above us. Instead, I look down and see clouds ringed with a silvery-jade outline, shades of green and blue rippling across them faster than a vapor can move in the air. Then the lightning comes, and my fingers grip the armrests of my chair as a blue-green crackle blasts from the cloud to the wingtip, which against all probability straightens out the plane. I can see the propeller by my window encased in a cylinder of lightning, spinning like a Tesla coil gone mad. My head whips over my shoulder and Pierre is quiet, almost meditative. I must be losing my mind with fear because I can see small sparks of green-tinted electricity escaping from his nostrils, then every pore and follicle of his body sparking lightning. As the electrical shell encases him, his body jerks, his eyes snap open, and for an instant his skin flashes like a firefly.

* * *

Pierre Maschinot is nothing but a con artist. He met me at a restaurant attached to a golf club in Shawinigan and didn't even eat.

He was kind enough to listen to me describe my investigation: the discrepancies in the forensic reports, the fuselage sections impossible to account for, the inexplicable clicking noises in the black box recording. At this last point, about the clicking, it was the only moment in our conversation when his smug demeanor seemed to crack. For an instant, Maschinot was serious, attentive, perhaps even a little afraid. It is possible that I've stumbled onto something I was never supposed to know. I never mentioned the strange electromagnetic activity I discovered through the NORAD data. Yet just mentioning these clicking noises was enough to make him suspicious. Initially, he fed me the same obviously false story that I had heard over email and phone conversations with town officials in Seul-Coeur, but when I told him that I had heard this song before, he changed his attitude.

He told me in accented and broken English that he understood my determination. Coming here from Massachusetts demonstrated that clearly enough, as far as he was concerned. But Seul-Coeur was a place that distrusted outsiders, especially outsiders who asked questions. That was true of so many small towns that it was impossible to fault any particular one. Yet every small town, no matter how much they hate outsiders, always encouraged the highways to move through when the opportunity came. Every town wants visitors as long as they bring enough money. Maschinot said I did not appear to have enough money to be welcome in Seul-Coeur, and he was certainly right on that detail. I even let myself laugh a little in front of him, until he said that the world's richest oil sheiks wouldn't have enough money to be welcome in his town. It made me wonder why he condescended to meet me. He said his town wouldn't let people in, but that he was willing to meet with some of those who would come from outside. Merely having learned enough English to have a conversation was a long distance farther than most of his neighbors would ever imagine going.

So why could I not go to Seul-Coeur? Because he was not the one making the decisions about who could enter the town, or ever settle there. I was no money grubber, no rapacious oilman, no public relations guru for a fracking or mining company. I only wanted to find out what happened to my wife. He tried to tell me that sometimes life really was that simple, that sometimes people just die. But I knew by now not to be tricked by his outwardly child-like truisms. Everything about this meeting stank of a cover-up.

He started to talk to me about grief, about his mother having left him a long time ago, how untimely it felt to him, completely out of his control, a change that he could only watch. Even watching, being with her as she was going through it was too much for him. At least he was able to say goodbye, which was more than I ever managed. He could acknowledge that the catharsis helped, that he believes he may see her again. It was not as shocking to him as losing Zoiey must have been for me. But at bottom, he said, loss was loss. It had been a long time since I had spoken to someone about loss. My friends are useless. My sister always hides from the conversation, making distractions, discussing any topic but the one she wants to avoid. My own daughter can no longer stand to walk inside my apartment because she thinks I've lost my mind. But then Maschinot asks me something for which I cannot forgive him.

If you do discover that there was more to your wife's death than a plane crash, he asks, what will you do? If you indeed reach the crash site, he asks, what will you be able to accomplish other than simply saying goodbye? His mouth was closed, but his jaw was slack like a frog, his eyes wide and almost naive as he waited for me to answer. As if he thinks anything practical about Zoiey's death matters. I have been unable to care about anything practical for the last twelve years. I thought he could understand, but by asking that question he shows how ignorant he really is. Truth is its own justification. Would he take me to Seul-Coeur or not?

The answer was *not*, it seems. He paid the bills for both our meals—including his untouched half-chicken dinner—had the gall to shake my hand, and left. He may not have said I could come to that twisted little town of his, nor given me any clue how to get there other than going in the general direction of north. But he will not see me give up that easily. Maschinot may have tried to discourage me, to throw me off, to deflate and demoralize me, but I am only more determined now to discover what he is hiding. I don't yet know how I will get there, or what I will do when I arrive. I have a car, a compass, and a set of maps, more than enough to reach Lac du Monarque, and Seul-Coeur on its shoreline. When I get there, I will find what Maschinot and the people of that town have been hiding from me. Their secrets will not be kept just because some huckster savant, probably the only one in the whole town who got a college education, tried to keep me from infiltrating their little clique.

* * *

Pierre tells me I passed out during the worst of the turbulence, the severe shocks and bumps exacerbated by several lightning strikes that came perilously close to us. "The experience is very different in a small plane." He murmurs about how fragile we are when flying in these small aircraft, and from the way he is speaking as I wake up, it's as if he'd been talking while I was still asleep. "There is only so much I could do to make ready, to prepare. Sometime, what will happen is unexpected, and I can only see a little bit of de future. The irony would have been too terrible if we lost control of de plane." As Pierre narrates these anxious meanderings, I watch the trees whiz by along the highway, trying to find a calm place in my thoughts to wait out the stomach pain I've had since our plane touched down at the "airport" in Rouyn-Noranda, a landing strip carved out of the woods. I stepped out of the plane to be knocked nearly unconscious by a wall of heat, a thick humidity apparently typical of Quebec's interior in the summer. Pierre had to help me the short distance from the tarmac to the parking lot.

I sit in his truck with the window rolled down, struggling to keep my eyes open, lids feeling as if they weigh pounds. The muscles of my eyes have been straining all day, but through blurred vision I can see Pierre by the airport entrance barking orders at the boys. The clean-shaven one nods his head and darts inside. Our adolescent pilots don't look at me with anger anymore, so I don't think I'm afraid of them any longer. But I find the boy with the mustache staring at me again with a gaze that is strangely worse than his anger from earlier this afternoon. He regards me with a pitiful contempt, thinks me too pathetic to earn his rage. They can have their contempt, these rustic children.

Our entire trip after leaving the town has been a blur of trees, as the dizzy spell that hit me during our turbulence has become the slow throbbing of a migraine. The trees, fading with our speed into a hazy green mass, have become indistinct even in their color as the sun has finally begun to set. I turn my head from what is now the most powerful source of light for miles, the headlights of Pierre's truck. I have never been on a road with no other cars, no guardrails, and so few streetlights. It's barely a highway—just a long, straight road, two lanes of pavement cutting through the trees with an embarrassed discretion, like the road didn't want to remind the trees that it existed.

There have been many times in my life where I felt isolated and alone, as though no one could understand my perspective or my history. Those times cover most of my life as an adult. Somehow, being physically isolated—Pierre and I the only humans within miles of opaque, sleeping forest—is not as damaging to me as those years when the requests of friends to come out and enjoy life, the pleas of family to help an old man recover from another breakdown, were constantly humming in the background. I had long given up on my father, as well as my friends who had no cares except school, and to whom men were only distractions from an empty life. There was no special path that led me to this place, only one event after another. Now I listen to the implausible excuses of a man whose fascinating weirdness and sincerity brought me here, trying to describe what happened today as ordinary turbulence. I should be terrified, but I've adjusted to this strangeness. The boys were frightening because they were threatening, raging, hostile. Yet contempt at least implies some minimal respect.

I open my eyes and the darkness of the trees has turned to a dull crimson, the needles of the evergreens burning a phosphorescent red, an otherworldly impossibility lighting our way home. My father wrote his journal and assembled his investigation materials with the dedication of a madman, convinced that there were hidden meanings and conspiracies behind every inexplicable event. When I first heard him speak about all this, I couldn't bear to listen to it, the ravings of an unhinged old coot. But there was a look in Pierre's eyes when we first met at dad's funeral, a look that perceived more than surfaces, that saw differently than I could. My eyelids open and close like the slow gasping of a goldfish mouth, and I drift in and out of sleep for the last hour of the truck ride, the crimson haze of the forest deepening into purple, curtains of glowing fuchsia and red threading around the trees like aurora borealis stretching out of the earth itself. I know now that I will experience many strange things here in Seul-Coeur, which in Boston, hiding from my father's illusions, I would never have dreamed existed. Anomalous colors have been a feature of drug trips and mystical visions for centuries, and what I am seeing could very well be a hallucination. Embedded in the fabric of that hallucination is Pierre's persistent rambling. I stopped paying attention to him long ago, so he is essentially talking to himself. He is still making excuses, still miserable over the pain caused to me during the flight. This is not the attitude of a malicious man, but perhaps of someone in over his head to the same degree I am. I don't need to suspect this man. He already has so much regret, and we just got here.

We arrive at Pierre's house about two hours after sunset, a farm without animals, with only a small personal plot of land amounting to no more than a vegetable garden. Though I could not see the rest of the land in the dark, he tells me the farm has mostly given itself over to a chaos of weeds and mosses. On his land's far northern border, he says I should be able to hear the bubbling intrusion of an underground tributary sneaking above the surface.

My room is a small den reorganized into something like a guest room. There are still a couple of boxes of old clothes, but the otherwise spartan room is lit by a skylight when the sun shines, and includes a sofa that Pierre is kind enough to open for me. He apologizes to me again for the turbulence, and I tell him that he has nothing to be sorry about. He allows his face to contort to a shape of severe panic, if only for an instant, before sliding back into his neutral sadness, and bids me goodnight in his guttural, blubbering accent.

The people of this town are trying to hide something that may have meant that my mother's last moments were probably bathed in green cloudlight with electricity dancing around jet engines. Perhaps that secret has to do with the odd clacking noises I hear faintly through the glass of the den's bay window, coming from that faraway forest edge whose trees are made invisible by a rural night unable to prevent secrets from slipping out.

3.

The clacking echoed through the window, the sound crawling about the rafters and crevices of Pierre's house, as if a noise could slink out of the cracks between floorboards and settle into the gap between my brain and skull. When I wake up just after sunrise, I'm unnerved at how well I slept, how quickly I've adjusted to uncanny sounds and to lights that are unlike anything human technology—or a human world—could create. At first I wrote off my father's scrawls as the delusions and ravings of an unhinged man, and refused to deal with him. I could not face insanity and maintain myself. Now that I can experience some of what he saw, his words and his journal make sense to me. I can only hope to endure better than he did what I might see.

A city like Boston is a place we've lit so brightly that nothing can exist there without human permission, or at least without having some role to play in a human world. But these woods stay dark even in the blush of sunrise, and glow crimson through the night. As I watch the forest through the window, I can imagine the terrors that exist there, foreign bodies incompatible with our concrete jungles. So much is unseen in the darkness that maybe we were right to chase the mystery away with our fences made of streetlights and power grids. I still fear what my father became, even more now that I've been where he was and can see what he saw. When I only had my father's madness and paranoia to face, I couldn't bring myself to accept his world. Now, I see. I face a world where forests glow a mix of indigo and plasma-red, where airplanes are enveloped in membranes of emerald electricity. I can hear a conduit of that impossible lightning stirring down the hall as Pierre fries something to eat. My mind should be broken, snapped by events and phenomena that human knowledge tells me should not exist. Even so, I pull on my socks and walk to breakfast.

Pierre is fully dressed, milling around a black metal woodstove whose pipe feeds up into the ceiling. Arranged around where the pipe meets the stove are two frying pans and a coffee pot. One pan is full of scrambled eggs, which he stirs every so often. The other contains a long fish whose position in the pan he constantly adjusts to keep its scales from sticking. When he watches the food, his cheeks and mouth sag as if his skin were about to flop off his face, but when he turns to say good morning, the skin pulls back, and he looks more human again. There is another window here in the kitchen, smaller than in the den, but the same forest is visible through it. The smell and the bubbling sound of cooking fish sets off some memory of last night, a distant memory, from when I was sleeping. I was in that forest, and I could hear a voice under the rising and falling clicks and clacks. The voice was almost as silent as a tear falling, but I could hear it, and I knew it. It was my father and mother, speaking with the same voice — entangled as one, somehow. The voice was utterly different from how my parents sounded individually, but I knew it was their voice. Then I was digging, first impotently at mud and clay, then tearing up layer after layer of sod, then overturning whole trees to find them. But I never found them, and the voice never went away. I wonder if the sound would return with the clicking if the crackles of Pierre's frying pan and the bubbling of his coffee pot were to stop, if everything except the forest were to fall silent. Maybe that was part of what snapped in Dad, that he started to think with the logic of the forest, the logic of a dream where everything fits together no matter how horrifying the whole picture might be.

But now it's time for a breakfast of fish, eggs, and coffee. I sit at an old table of metal and cheap plastic across from a man so weak that he could barely face me at my father's funeral, and yet is able to absorb an electrical storm in the cabin of that flying rat-trap he called an airplane.

Pierre tells me that most of the meals he eats are different kinds of fish he catches throughout the year at Lac du Monarque. "The peoples of our town have always had certain rights because no one ever thinks to come here to see if they can take them away from us." He laughs, a demonstration of the sense of humor this town and country share, both of which are still foreign to me. I remember a name from my father's research folders that described the people of Seul-Coeur, Métis, and I ask Pierre what it means. "Did I never tell you?" He had mentioned the word when we first met, but he never followed up.

A thousand years ago, he says, only Cree lived in this part of Canada. Then the first Europeans came. I thought he meant the British settlers, but apparently they never came this far north. "They stuck to your lands in America, and it took them long time to come inland." Instead, apparently, it was the French who came to the lakes of the interior, in the 1500s. And they did it without armies or politics or town councils or even families. They were fur trappers, all men and all alone. "They lived from the land just like Cree. They learned to speak Cree and Cree people learned to speak French. There was a lot more in common with French trappers and Cree than trappers had with French of Paris, Lyon, and Marseilles." The trappers were strange, pale foreigners from a land and culture utterly alien to the Cree, a land of noblemen, kings, and scientists. But the trappers and the Cree faced the same problems trying to live and thrive in a rugged land with a harsh winter. It only made sense that they became one people, and so they became the Métis. "The word in Français is simple, almost crude. I think it was originally an insult. It means mix... eyebred."

I contemplate the weightiness of the word—hybrid—and we sit in silence for a moment. Then, "Why did you bring me here, Pierre?"

He sighs, resigned to my asking the question because he is anticipating it at this precise moment in our collaboration. I was here because Seul-Coeur could not isolate itself any longer, "at least as far as I am concerned," he says. Reflection on the few conversations he had with my father convinced Pierre that the town's policy of secrecy, especially around the plane crash, was no longer productive, and was doing more harm than good. Eventually, outsiders will come.

So with my father's presence, Pierre saw an opportunity to initiate change. "Not everybody agree with me, of course." That much was plain from the way our pilots looked at me in the airport hangar in Montreal yesterday. I still feel fear at the contempt in that one boy's eyes. "Jean-Claude is a difficult boy. But he is a good pilot. That is why he flies the planes for few times Seul-Coeur people visit the cities. But he is a difficult boy. The most difficult boy." I wonder what makes him difficult, and Pierre tells me that it's no more than the troubles that face every teenage boy, when the only appropriate response to anything is anger. "I was a lot like him when I was his age. Not so long ago, maybe."

"What did you have to be angry about?" I ask, my voice muffled by a mouthful of fish.

His eyes look away from me. Lost in a memory, he looks less human than I've ever seen him. I'm tense, his next actions a mystery. But Pierre only speaks. "It is simpler than you would think." His gaze settles first on his coffee mug, and after he takes a drink his eyes meet mine. "I was young when my mother was gone. Younger than Jean-Claude is now, but not by much." I know that a teenager, whether man or woman, who loses a parent often has nowhere to go. She's convinced that her pain is incomprehensible, alien to everyone but herself, and sometimes even to herself. She turns inward, away from anyone who might help her and against anyone whose help she might need.

I ask Pierre if he still has his father, but the answer is no. Once his mother had gone, he had the entire farm to look after himself, which is why it grew so much smaller in the last two decades, despite the hard work he put into it over the first few years. As a young man, it was common for him to work for fifteen or sixteen hours during the day, sometimes without a single day off for weeks. This was the pattern of his life for years, until he could no longer bear the repetitions of planting, harvest, and winter cycles. As he started losing focus on the farm, he began teaching himself simple English from watching the few television channels in my language that were available this far north. "I knew some people in town who were upset with me, resented me, when I let the farm go so I could attend university in Rouyn-Noranda. I was... I was tired of the attitude that we must not leave town. I knew it was wrong, but I could not say why. I was young and angry. So I left in order to learn the *why*, and maybe to discover the reasons for my feeling."

"Did you learn the *why?*" I find Pierre's phrasing somewhat comical at times, but intriguing, poetic. Pierre tells me that he learned a lot at university—the English language, philosophy and literature in both the languages he could speak, the science of farming, and a little physics. But with respect to his mother and father, "I still do not know that I understand the absence. I could only feel like... I could only feel something like a clue when I first saw you last week. When you think of your parents, I can sense that your eyes are the same as mine."

* * *

Simply finding this town was a nightmare, and I expect this nightmare will not end until I can leave again. I should expect this of the wilderness, but my soul is still too used to the symmetrical lines of cities and streets laid out on grids. That is the weakness of humanity: we have grown too accustomed to our own order. When the daily routines are upset, too often we are thrown into depression and madness. The small jeep I rented for the voyage has been loaded down with cans of gas in case I get lost a few too many times. I eventually fulfilled my own prediction there. The trees enveloped me for days, and I was side-tracked driving down dirt roads that ended at the shorelines of lakes, or at sheer cliff faces. But at last I arrived at the shore of Lac du Monarque, and my binoculars revealed the malevolent profile of Seul-Coeur outlined against thick woods and a leaden sky dense enough to erase the sun. This town hides even light.

I drove my jeep into the edge of a small clearing, parked it behind a random tree, and covered it in fallen foliage. It was a pathetic way to hide a vehicle, but I could think of no other means. My half-hearted camouflage done, I hoisted my backpack on and began the walk along the lakeshore to Seul-Coeur. At this distance the walk would last through the night, but I was not tired, having napped at hiatuses in my driving throughout the arduous journey here from Shawinigan—and I vowed not to sleep until I discovered the mystery behind this town and the plane crash that destroyed Zoiey.

I knew that Seul-Coeur lies on the north shore of the lake, and I stopped my jeep on the south shore. In spite of the effort to isolate themselves, even these people cannot hide for much longer from Google Earth. There are mountains along the western shore, so I decided to walk the longer route along the eastern shore, keeping the lake on my left. As long as I stay within sight of the lake, and as long as the lake is on my left, I will reach that town of tricksters well before I exhaust my supply of canned food and bottled water. If necessary I will take a drink from the lake, but I still cannot trust the environment here. I have studied the electromagnetic phenomena of this region in too much detail to be convinced that there is not a single substance within this haunted landscape that has not been touched by it. My plan to infiltrate the town was simple enough and, in my mind, could never have gone wrong. I stuck to the planned route and it indeed took as long as I had estimated. But I can no longer allow myself to sleep in these woods after what I saw and heard.

Night fell late on the eastern shore of Lac du Monarque, an effect of the approaching summer solstice. I have been used to camping my entire life, and have always loved the feeling of open lonesomeness and the sight of stars unobscured by the glare from city lights. My favorite memories as a boy were of nights at the rundown old hovel that my uncle Murray used to call a cottage. It was located in small-town Vermont near a long-abandoned brewery. The sun would sink and make monstrous shadows out of the disjointed brick castle. Then the lights would disappear, and the brewery would fade into the same forest where I could hear the crickets, nighthawks, and owls singing and calling—a true American gothic scene. I would fall asleep in my uncle's long backyard bathed in a fragrance of sweet pine. That same smell surrounded me last night, and was the only thing that allowed me to keep my sanity. I knew with every breath that I was still in the world of pine and spruce, the same world where I grew up, a world like Vermont.

Yet my eyes and ears betrayed me. The sounds were the first thing that kept me from sleep, a clicking that began faintly at first, then slowly grew in volume as I lay in my sleeping bag. I tried to think of a sound that it reminded me of—a demented tap-dancer, a telegraph machine hit with a power surge, the rattling of dice in a cylindrical container, the perpetual fracturing of bones. None of these could explain it. The sound had no rhythm, but instead an irregular pattern of unpredictably shifting frequencies and machine gun beats, fading away from one direction before rising again from another. East then west, north then east, then south, northwest, and once even from directly below me. The clacking kept me awake, kept my mind unsettled.

Then the light started, faintly at first, an odd violet haze that I could talk myself into believing was the last gleam of dying sunset filtering through the trees. But light is not supposed to grow brighter in the night. The glow crept up on me, slowly growing in intensity as the twilight retreated into the horizon. Suddenly I could not distinguish where the glow of twilight ended and the radiance of the forest began. I could make out the light moving in waves across the trees, as if the pine and spruce needles were generating a purple luminance that traveled from branch to branch, spire to spire, in arcs jagged like lightning that unraveled sluggishly but elegantly. Purple light rested in the needles of the trees, burning their otherworldly cold heat into my retinas. I spent the night shaking and shuddering, even though it was the height of spring. Horror has the power to strike chills into a man as deep as his marrow. I tried to work out some pattern, some correlation between the changes in the lights and the clicking. It was a move of desperation, a last resort to keep my thoughts focused on something other than the haze emanating from the trees, the alien ghost of the forest manifested. These lights were not just unnatural. They were anti-natural, a force that transformed the peace of a forest at night into an otherworldly terror. But the sound and light seemed not to impact each other at all—which only made them more terrifying. Not only was I surrounded by forces from a world of monsters, but there was not any discernible order to it, no purpose, no underlying law or constancy. Zoiey, my love. You must have died filled with fear.

* * *

I don't know if I have ever seen the sun as bright as I have this morning. Pierre is driving me to the central town of Seul-Coeur, no more than five or six streets, including the roads that lead to the farms to the north and the marina to the south. We drive in silence because we both hate the music that's played on the radio. "Montreal pop and tired ol' folk music," he tells me, and it's all terrible. While we're laughing about the universal uselessness of FM radio, I avoid looking directly at his face, not wanting to see what odd shapes the muscles might make as he speaks. I focus my eyes on the road, and keep my sunglasses propped on my nose to prevent the excessive summer sunlight from ruining my vision. Despite the intense sunlight, these woods bordering the road are still dark.

We are going to the mayor's office, a man whose name I have yet to figure out how to pronounce. The road passes out of the denser forests again, and I see small farms, decaying barns, and rusting windmills standing isolated among feral pastures and irregularly shaped bales of hay. These images are slightly more human than what I've experienced since yesterday. I wonder if the otherworldly aspects of this town only appear at night to hover in the hidden crevices of the forest, or to float in cloud patches thousands of feet in the air. Then I glance at Pierre, and I'm not sure if it's an effect of the glare on the edge of my sunglasses, but the muscles under his cheeks are creeping

~ 57 ~

in odd patterns again. It's a reminder that he—along with everything in the vicinity of Seul-Coeur, for that matter—is something other than human. But when I look at him, I don't feel the fear, rage, or revulsion that my father described in his journals. I've seen Pierre try to hide the pain in his eyes when he talks about his mother. Whatever secrets he's still keeping from me, I can't be afraid of him. He's my friend.

Even though the streets of this town appear normal, I am always a little on edge wondering when the next fluorescent firestorm is going to ignite, dancing on the unseen molecules linking Pierre's body to the deceptively benign atmosphere. The houses are far apart, some needing a new coat of paint. But nothing is truly run-down—not like in the small towns I've driven through in upstate New York and parts of Pennsylvania and Ohio, where everything is a living picture of decay happening in real time. Though some of these older houses appear to be coated with a thin layer of dust, Seul-Coeur seems to have more life in it than many of the towns I've visited for work. For a couple of years, my boss would look for old housing districts in smaller towns to repair and sell to young families or landlords. We could never find enough small communities with a growing population or business investment to put our own money into. Those were the depressing times at my job, when every month or so I would drive out to some part of America that had no future but to become a crumbling heap of broken dreams. If I had seen more towns like Seul-Coeur, those projects would have given me an inexplicable kind of hope.

We're approaching what looks to be the business district of the town (or whatever the business district of a five-street town would be), a small cluster of three-story brick buildings in the typical Main Street style, and a clock tower at the intersection of two of the streets. We enter the cluster and pull into a parking lot fringed by a carefully manicured garden, its bushes evenly spaced and pruned to look like simple geometric figures: rectangles, pyramids, spheres. The shapes of the plant sculptures are almost laughably simple, as if over-compensating for the chaos I suspect this town hides. There is a gardener inspecting his work, making a few small adjustments to a tree pruned into a steeply sloping cone. He's bald but young, or at least middle-aged, with a ring of dark hair around the back of his head that has gone too long without a pruning of its own. His skin is the same ruddy copper as Pierre's.

My slamming the truck door makes him turn his head to examine the new arrivals. The gardener returns Pierre's wave with a nod of respect, yet when he sees me, his face hardens into a hostile glare. Despite the distance I can see muscles moving underneath his forehead in abnormal patterns. I'm glad that I've grown used to this bizarre disturbance rumbling beneath the faces of Seul-Coeur folk. Now it's just a sign of a person's origin, and not the disturbing flux of the unnatural that unnerved me when I first met Pierre barely a week ago. All that disturbs me about this strange aspect of my friend's appearance is that it took me a week to get used to it.

As we walk away from the steel-eyed gardener toward the central building of the town square, Pierre tells me that the mayor of Seul-Coeur is one of his oldest friends. So it was no problem for him to discuss the idea of meeting me briefly just to show that, despite some of my father's beliefs, there is nothing particularly sinister about Seul-Coeur. "We are a town that likes to be left alone. Sometimes we like it too much. Mayor Bosaygla feels similar to me, if for different reasons."

"Every small town has its secrets," I say. "Most towns, the secrets are no worse than who's having an affair with whom, and who's really the father of the schoolteacher's new baby."

"That does happen here sometimes."

I smile at his candor, and at his strange politeness in holding the door open for me as we enter the town hall. "Jean-Marie is a typical mayor. He thinks about the economy and the internet. I think the English term is *buzzword*?" I tell him it is, and that I know exactly the kind of small-town politician he's describing. I've seen so many of them, even in a town as "small" as Boston, that I almost think I know how to handle this one. Of course, I also know I'll see muscles and blood vessels shifting under his facial skin. I finally ask Pierre for the precise pronunciation of the mayor's last name, because I have no idea what word comes out of his mouth when he says it.

"Bosaygla. Simple." I pause in the foyer, cock my head to the side, and tap my foot, clacking regularly on the floor to remind him without words that I have little idea how his language works. Finally he asks me to take my iPad out of my bag so he can write it for me. I call up the note-taking app, make a new sheet, and pass it to him. When he returns it to me a moment later, I can read the word "Beauseigle," and am amazed how that pronunciation comes out of a name that looks to me like it should sound like Bo-Seagull. Pierre tells me I should have paid more attention in school, turns away, and leads me down a corridor whose sickly green carpet is only one part of a painfully outdated design. It doesn't surprise me that this town hall's decor hasn't been updated from the style a conservative bureaucrat would have chosen in 1967, the walls a sickly gray-green and the lighting barely effective. I expect to meet several small-town bureaucrats today, bizarre neo-cons who may also be otherworldly creatures crackling with electricity. However, for now I concentrate on following Pierre down the correct corridors to the mayor's office.

I should have expected disappointment, as when we reach Mayor Seagull's office, no one is there but his secretary. She and Pierre have a spirited conversation in extremely fast French. At first, I can work out fragments of what Pierre is saying when he asks where the mayor is. Then I'm lost. The secretary is a severely dressed young woman, with a complexion slightly lighter than Pierre's but still coppery, and a globe of frizzy, upright hair that's utterly incompatible with her tightly buttoned and featureless blouse. She points her pen at me in a jabbing motion enough times in the conversation that I know I should feel uncomfortable. Pierre stands between me and the secretary, defending me again from a threat that I can't understand. At last he throws up his hands, utterly losing his temper at the secretary who responds with nothing more than a callous smirk. He shouts loud enough to be heard outside, and I'm glad I can't see what distorted shapes are roiling beneath his face.

At this, he takes my hand and leads me out of the office. "Come, Marilyn! We are leaving! There is nothing for us here!" He's dragging me behind him, and I'm so surprised by the jerk of his hand that it's all I can do to keep from falling down and ruining his climactic exit. As he storms down the corridor, I demand to know what the hell was going on in that office. Pierre shoves the building door so hard as we leave that he nearly shatters its glass. Once we're in the parking lot, he's finally calmed down enough to tell me. "Jean-Marie promise me he would meet us at his office. Now he does de same to me dat I was order to do to Pauls!"

Pierre's hair looks as if it's about to stand on end, its roots animated by a force driving them upright, pulling against the gravity of his hair gel. I involuntarily step back. He seems to notice this and calms down, asking for a moment to himself, rubbing his eyes under his glasses, then turning his back to me. He takes a couple of steps toward the truck, breathes deeply, and I see Pierre raise his arm to look at his watch. "I know where he is." We walk to the truck, and as I sit down he tells me that the mayor has gone to an early lunch, but that he will be at the place he always goes, a restaurant called Fredrick. It's apparently the only restaurant in Seul-Coeur, and the seagull mayor eats there every day.

"But if he's trying to avoid you," I ask, "wouldn't he go somewhere you wouldn't expect to find him?"

For an ordinary person, according to Pierre, that would be true. He would go home, or visit a friend, or go somewhere he knew the person he was hiding from didn't like to go. That's How to Avoid People 101. But Seul-Coeur is a small town. Everyone has known everyone since birth, and Pierre knew Jean-Marie Seagull better than anyone else did. "I tell you something about Jean-Marie. He can be an idiot." I laugh as Pierre starts the truck, backs out of the parking space, and turns onto the street. The mayor, apparently, does not deal with stress well, and taking me to Seul-Coeur has introduced more stress in his life than he had ever experienced before. When Mayor Seagull is under stress, he apparently must relax immediately, which means going to where he feels most comfortable. "That means his favorite table at Shay Fredrick. It's even in sight of their biggest window."

The restaurant isn't far, so I ask why we don't just walk. Pierre says it isn't a good idea for me to walk outside right now, whether on my own or with him. No one here knows me, he says, but everyone here knows who I am. I'm not about to let him get away without explaining that, so he parks the truck about fifty feet down the road from the restaurant and turns off the engine. He lowers his forehead to rest on the steering wheel, and his arms hide from me the inhumanly sagging skin around his mouth and jaw. Pierre asks if my father ever described his last trip to Seul-Coeur. We never spoke of it, I reply. During his last three years, we never spoke at all, certainly never about Quebec or the plane crash. I don't tell Pierre that I've been reading dad's journals.

So Pierre describes to me, slowly, haltingly, that my father showed up in Seul-Coeur several days after their meeting in the Shawinigan restaurant three years ago, and what he said and did offended a lot of people. After that incident, the town was divided over what should be done. Some wanted further secrecy, even cutting off the regular propeller plane flights to Rouyn-Nor

anda and breaking economic links with surrounding towns. Others thought like Pierre, wanting to open up the town, knowing that further secrecy would only encourage more people to risk their lives to uncover what was hidden in Seul-Coeur. Pierre and many of his friends knew that the status quo was unsustainable, that the culture of the town would have to change. They would have to get creative if they wanted to be left alone.

"After the funeral, I spend all night on the phone with Jean-Marie and many of my friends in Seul-Coeur. You are our first experiment in opening the town. There are many who want the experiment to fail." Some people in Seul-Coeur have lived isolated for decades, treasure that isolation, and will do whatever they can to defend it. Now I realize just how much danger I am in. There are people in Seul-Coeur who regard me as an invading pathogen, and are willing to do what is necessary to neutralize me before I can return to Boston.

"Go to the restaurant," I tell him. I came to Seul-Coeur on my own, and no matter the fear, I can't back down now. "Talk with the mayor. If it's okay for me to join you, text me to say so and I'll walk up to the restaurant. If it isn't okay, I'll wait here until you come back."

Pierre stares out the windshield, deep in thought. Now his skin is pulled inhumanly tight, and his hair is pulling itself upward again. When he looks at me, I can see through his glasses the steel seriousness in his eyes. "When I am sure what is happening, I will send you a text with one letter. E to come to the restaurant and sit down with us. R for stay here." He takes the keys from the ignition and puts them in my hand. At this, I feel my heart beating faster. "If I text you A, take the truck and run. Back to the farm as fast as you can. Lock the doors and wait for me." As I think through precisely what the latter instructions imply, I don't know if I can keep calm enough to carry out any of Pierre's directives. Before he goes, I ask him one last question. Why those letters?

At last the tension is broken, and Pierre laughs at me again for my total ignorance of French. E is for entray, or enter. I can tell that much. R is for restay, which apparently means stay. A is for allay, which means go. He takes my hand and wraps my fingers around his keys, promising me he will not take long. I'm not shaking or anything obvious like that, but I wonder if Pierre can detect my nervousness through my rapid heartbeat.

And so I simply breathe, waiting for the signal, and remembering these few words in my newest French lesson. Enter. Stay. Go. Entrer. Rester. Aller. I twitchily finger Pierre's keys, turning them over in my hand, feeling the bumps and shapes. There's the big truck key, three keys for the house's back door, front wooden door, and front storm door. Then the key to the barn, a barn with no animals in it, that hasn't had animals for years. And a couple of keys with no purpose that I know of. A shed? A storage locker somewhere in town or in Rouyn-Noranda?

My phone sits in my lap, my heart still beating with an uneasy rhythm. I'm thinking about how the desire for isolation doesn't make someone threaten a woman, look at her with violence and contempt like the aggression in that pilot boy's eyes. All women fear walking in darkness—the gloved hand on a wrist, being dragged into an alley where the only light is the reflection from a knife blade. That fear is palpable enough in a city at night, or even when alone with someone you don't quite trust yet. It's a nagging question, a sensation of uncertainty, the faint yet regular ticking of a watch. You've gone too long without violence happening to you, so now it's your turn. There are people in this town with secrets held so dearly that they might be willing to kill for them, and who might have done something to my father to turn him into the wreck he became in his last few years. That much, now, is undeniable. I have to accept that there are people around here, maybe even watching the truck right now, who would do the same to me. My father may have been their victim, but I won't be taken so easily, no matter what kinds of horrors are buried under this town. Not all of what dad described in his journal could have been hallucinations and dreams. The trick will be disentangling the delirium from the reality. I knew from the start that I wouldn't have help sorting that out. Pierre has been trying to pacify my incessant questions through empathetic responses, but that's not the same as answering them. I have to accept that there might be people in Seul-Coeur who will actively try to silence me. There are many ways to silence someone in the middle of the woods.

I let a yelp escape when my phone vibrates in my lap. Just one letter, like he said. E for entrer. Enter. Welcome. Come on in. At least one person wants me here, now maybe even two. But just because the mayor doesn't mind me sitting down with him doesn't mean he wants to help me. This may be just the first step in shutting me up. Either way, I've been summoned, so I go.

I drop Pierre's keys in my purse, step onto the sidewalk, close the heavy truck door and walk to the restaurant. I see Pierre and the mayor, Jean-Marie, talking. They are framed perfectly by the restaurant's huge plate-glass window, and I do not understand how anyone could think it would be effective to hide in plain view of everyone on the street. Jean-Marie is agitated, making large, manic gestures with his arms. His forehead is high, and his thinning hair stands uncontrollably on end. Pierre, meanwhile, sits with his arms folded, shaking his head. His mouth barely opens to speak, so he must be the quiet one. I can see who's in charge. And now, I am clearly in charge of this conversation, because both of them have stopped talking and are staring at me as I look at them, equally visible through a wall-sized window.

I scurry inside and sit next to Pierre, my back to the window so that I can see most of the restaurant's interior—a surprisingly sprawling space when considering the size of the town. Rent per square foot must be cheap in Seul-Coeur. The mayor has been talking just as loudly as he looked from outside, his French with a deeper accent than Pierre's. When I sit down, though, he shuts up. Pierre introduces me, which I know because my name sounds the same in French and English. The mayor is deflated, though. "Je say, je say, je comprawn," he repeats, and then noisily exhales. They talk further, Jean-Marie seeming to plead with his defiant guest. Pierre can only shake his head, a refusal to accept what the mayor tells him, speaking calmly and quietly over hands tightly clasped, almost praying. But Pierre isn't asking anything, I can tell, as you would in prayer. His words are statements, declarations with an eloquence that I can hear without understanding. Above all, I can hear his disappointment in his friend the mayor. I've never known anyone for as long as Pierre and the mayor have known each other, so intimately and continuously in the same small town. I can feel them splitting apart, a rift opening in the table like an ice floe breaking in two, drifting away from each other on diverging currents. They speak volumes in language that only sounds to me like a friendship collapsing in gibberish, years of intimacy and friendship deepening or deflecting the meaning of every word exchanged. Jean-Marie sits with his eyes closed, rubbing his fingers against his forehead, his face hidden by his hand. I try to whisper a question to Pierre, wondering what they have been discussing.

"You should not bee eer! You should not ave come!" I'm speechless now, shocked, my jaw hanging open like an idiot. Jean-Marie has banged the table so hard with his fist that a spoon has jumped off and clattered on the floor. Water breaches the rim of his glass and spills onto a plate. One of my hands grips the edge of the table. The other finds itself on Pierre's leg, hidden from sight under the tablecloth. The mayor shows me more of his hidden English. "You do not unnerstan! You never unnerstan! Only oo live eer all er life can unnerstan! You are alien! Outside! My mistake was ave Pierre do dis! Ave Pierre bring you." He's choking with childish tears, snorting from the excess mucus. He wipes his face with a napkin, but it does no good. It only brings out the darkening circles under his eyes. His mouth is twisted into an unnatural shape. He has lost all self-control, all because I sat down and whispered a question so I could understand something of what was happening around me.

Pierre stands and approaches his oldest friend, placing a hand on his shoulder and imploring him in French to calm down.

"No! No!" he bawls, knocking his hand away. "Zhna puh pwain! Zhna puh jammay." Jean-Marie is throwing a tantrum in his chair. I've never seen a grown man so out of control, and it reminds me of how I howled alone in my room when they told me my mother was dead. "Je temploah. Keyteh mwa donk je swee sul. Zhna puh pah voo regarday," he tells us both. He looks up into Pierre's eyes and asks, "Zhna puh pah te regarday. Keyteh mwa. Keyteh mwa." All Jean-Marie can do is repeat these last two words. I don't understand their meaning, but I know what he wants. Only now do I look around me and feel the glares of the other patrons. Literally everyone in the restaurant is staring at us. They've stopped eating, put down their forks and knives, let their coffee and tea cool. Even the waiter has stopped moving from table to table and stands by the entrance to the kitchen, watching us. No, they're watching me.

I tell Pierre we should go, and only when he hears my voice does he look away from his friend to see the eyes on us, glares, stares, hexes and snarls. I can barely see the faces, and only feel the hostility, the threats, the violence these eyes want to do me. Pierre sees something even worse. These are his people, his friends, the people of his home, and they're directing at him the same rage they are at me. Jean-Marie's blubbering is the only sound in the restaurant. Pierre puts a $20 bill on the table and leads me, wordlessly, outside. When we reach the truck, I ask him if there is anywhere in Seul-Coeur where we won't be stared at. He offers no response.

We drive around the town in silence, which doesn't take long because the town, as I've said, is a very small one. We pull into a public park near where the buildings thin into fields and gardens. A few small booths are set up, staffed by bored young men and women selling vegetables and preserves. We stop the truck and walk among their benches and stalls, and Pierre can finally speak. "I did not expect what you saw just now." I hardly thought he was expecting it. The mayor's outburst was exactly what I wouldn't have expected after getting the signal to come into the restaurant. They had spent a long time talking before I came in, summing up almost their entire friendship from the time they were toddlers until now. "We had relied on each other for so long that I never realize how he could feel so betrayed."

We stroll in circles going over what they said to each other, Pierre still rattled by what appeared to be the end of his longest friendship. The young girls and old women of the marketplace are watching us because they know Pierre—and they must, by the simplest deduction, know me as well. He grows repetitive, some sentences not always intelligible. I know by now that when he is under stress, Pierre forgets parts of his English and sometimes even slips completely into French as if I wasn't there beside him. From what I can gather, during my father's visit to Seul-Coeur, Pierre and Jean-Marie began the first of a long series of conversations about how outsiders can discover the town. They were no fools, and knew that in an era of the internet, satellites, and cables threaded across the continent, the affairs of Seul-Coeur couldn't be kept secret, and more incidents like my father's visit would occur.

I ask him just what the secrets of Seul-Coeur are, but he only answers with more stories about him and Jean-Marie. "He was first of both of us to suggest that I go to Boston and talk with Pauls. I am still the only person in this whole town who can have a full conversation in English." But Jean-Marie began to have doubts when, as Pierre was preparing to leave for Boston, he discovered in the online editions of the city's newspapers that my father had died. At that point, as far as Jean-Marie was concerned, the entire point of Pierre's trip to the United States had evaporated. Only then did Pierre understand his friend's motives for the visit. "We were not fair to Pauls when he was here. Jean-Marie wanted only to repay him. For me, it is about the future of Seul-Coeur." When I ask how Jean-Marie read English-language newspapers if his skills with my language were so limited, the answer is simple. "Google Translate," he says, laughing. The laughter continues longer than it should, a desperate expiration of air that deflates the man. Pierre pauses on the edge of suffocation, eyes staring forward, and then deeply inhales. He asks for a moment alone, and I let him take a walk to the edge of the farmers' market on his own.

I'm standing by a small tent occupied by a girl, no more than twenty years old, who is selling bunches of carrots and beets and bushels of cauliflower. She, like everyone else in this town, is staring at me, but I'm for once relieved that there seems to be no anger in her eyes. I ask her if she speaks any English. She says what sounds like "A bit," then asks "why?" I laugh, unsure if I should be embarrassed, or if the girl is playing a game with me. Even though I ask her if she knows who I am, I know she does, and she's honest enough to confirm it. She doesn't seem to mind that I'm here, at her stand or in her town, and seems content to talk to me. I ask her how old she is, and after I phrase the question in a couple of different ways, she understands. "Deeznuf… um, nineteen." I manage to figure out that she comes here most days to sell vegetables from her own farm, near the forest closer to the lakeshore. Asking if she is a farmer herself, she responds, "I… I live in de farm." In part, I wish Pierre was beside me to translate my words so I can be understood in this place. But I'm also pleased to be making what progress I can on my own. We both seem to be inwardly laughing at our inability to make sense of each other, which is at least an improvement over the restaurant incident. It's even an improvement over being with Pierre, who at the moment is sulking beside some droopy trees. When I ask her if she really knows who I am, she smiles and says, "Boston Girl." It's true, but I still have to tell her my name. "Allo, Marilyn. My name Rejeanne."

Since she knows who I am, I also ask her if she has any idea why I'm here. She knows who my father is, but describes him only as the man from the woods, or the man from Boston. She even thinks she knows why this woodsman was here: to find out what happened when the plane crashed during the lights in the sky. So I ask her about these lights, but they're ordinary to her, and she can't understand why I'd be so interested in them. I realize that she has never left Seul-Coeur in her life, and she confirms that she's never been beyond the eastern shore of Lac du Monarque. Rejeanne doesn't seem to understand that these lights, whatever they are, never occur anywhere outside Seul-Coeur. To her, this was a town no different from any other.

Still, she doesn't seem too curious even about the airplane crash. To her it was a strange event recalled from childhood, the timeless impressions of a toddler watching alien strangers scurrying around the forest. There was an explosion one night that all the town could hear, followed by the sensation that something had gone terribly wrong.

Then, within a few days, men appeared with foreign cars and strange technology conducting weird activities in the forest. The few times she saw one of these men, forensic investigators or police officers or government officials, she was frightened because of the way they moved. These men walked quickly and wordlessly, animated by a strong purpose. People in Seul-Coeur, she says, don't move this way. They take their time, relax, knowing that nothing is too urgent. They didn't seem like happy people, these urgent men, and the young Rejeanne was glad when they had gone. I ask for her phone number, because I'd like to talk to her later on, after Pierre feels better, so we could discuss things in more detail. But her farm has no land line, and she owns no cell phone. Still, she will be here selling what vegetables she can every day until Sunday. If I come back in the morning, I'll find her here at the market. Now more people are starting to arrive, and I recognize some of them as angry faces from the restaurant. I say one more goodbye to Rejeanne before trotting to Pierre so he can take me back to the truck.

"If it is okay with you," he says as we climb inside, "I would like to go back to the farm for a while. Today did not go as planned." It doesn't take us long to reach the road again, threading between the farmers' fields and forest canopies that have grown familiar to me, even though I have been here only a day. Pierre looks a wreck, less human than ever, as if he had just lost his best friend and doesn't care about maintaining appearances. He no longer has to adjust himself to a strange world. I'm the stranger here. We pass the rest of the drive in silence.

I spend the afternoon alone with my father's journal, trying to connect some of his raving to what I've actually experienced over the past two days. The electrical firestorms and otherworldly lights are what we agree on, but I've seen such a complicated town. In his journal, Pierre is a liar and the townspeople are freaks and monsters hunting my father down. Even after the strange phenomena I've experienced here, I have trouble believing some of the encounters he describes. I've seen people that frighten me—that restaurant full of seething stares, that withered gardener whose head I remember being almost egg-shaped, the fiery anger of our pilot Jean-Claude. But I've also seen empathy, namely, my host's apologies for the way he treated dad. And I've seen a man break down crying, backing away from a future that terrified him too much. Monsters don't cry. Monsters aren't naive teenagers selling vegetables in an outdoor market. Just a town, she called it, with no knowledge of other towns, no idea that Seul-Coeur is the only town where the trees glow crimson and purple at night.

Pierre and I sit in his living room at opposite ends of his long wicker and wood sofa. He's made us a simple dinner of rye bread and bowls of rice. I've been mulling over how to ask him about today, and I think I have the appropriate opening question.

"How did you feel when you first left Seul-Coeur?" His eyes widen, and for a moment he looks lost in memory. He talks about his excitement, the fluttering of his heart as he walked through the halls and pathways of the university campus at Rouyn-Noranda for the first time. He always felt different from everyone else throughout his time there—neither white nor Métis. But for the first time, he saw how large his own world was, a strange feeling for him.

"I read about Tibet people once," says Pierre, "that they have a special sense of the scale of the universe. Because they live at the top of the Himalayas for thousands of years, they have become customed to emptiness. A strange feeling for humans. All it takes to see the infinite is to look up." He wasn't really looking at me now, but his eyes seemed unfocused, staring after a distant place and time. "Seul-Coeur people feel the same way, but about our forest. We can see the infinite between the trees. Under the trees." But when I ask him why the forest is this way—why *this* forest and not any other forests, why *this* town and not any of the thousands of small towns scattered across the United States and Canada—he says that he can't really say, can't solidly put his finger on the difference.

"Or maybe you won't tell me."

"That is not fair, Marilyn." His face is tense now. I've stuck into him good. I don't know what's so unfair about it, because I dropped out of my own life and concerns to come here for answers about my mother and father, and all I've experienced are contradictions and hostility. A mayor bawling like a little boy, a series of enraged townspeople who look at me as though I should be strangled just for being here, and one naive girl who thinks there is nothing unusual about this place at all. "A girl? Who was that?" I can't believe he never noticed my fifteen-minute conversation with the girl at the farmers' market this afternoon. Her name was Rejeanne, and she was the only person in this town other than Pierre who's spoken to me with any friendliness.

"Were you so self-absorbed that you didn't notice I wasn't right beside you like I have been—pretty much non-stop—for the past few days?" He tells me again that what I say isn't fair to him, that he had just gone through the most catastrophic fight of his life with a man he's known since before they could walk properly. As upsetting as that is, Pierre has forgotten or ignored a lot that has remained in the front of my own thoughts. I remind him that the reason why he and Jean-Marie fought, why I came to Seul-Coeur with him, and why my father so obsessively tracked down this community (and every sordid detail about its dirty laundry) was that in 1997 a plane crashed at the edge of this town under circumstances that no scientific method could explain. My mother was on that plane. I was seventeen, and I lost a parent. That loss made an impact, and the resulting shockwave was manifested in the long, slogging decline of my father over more than a decade. "Seul-Coeur owes me the truth, and you promised me the truth."

"Marilyn, you do not understand," says Pierre. "I cannot make you understand what is outside your experience." I'm not listening to his excuses anymore. He can't write off those electrical disturbances when we were flying from Montreal as simple turbulence and bad weather.

I've been in thunderstorms before, and the lightning doesn't turn emerald.

"And as far as I know, a French-Indian half-breed doesn't conduct electricity better than any other human. But you could handle it just fine." He has no right to tell me what I can and can't understand. Pierre is standing now, towering over me as I'm sitting on the sofa in bare feet, gripping my empty rice bowl. His face is obscured, because the only light in the room comes from the setting sun behind him. I can't tell whether or not it's an effect of the light, but his silhouette seems to change shape, bulges emerging from his head and traveling down his torso.

When he and Jean-Marie first broached the idea of asking an outsider to visit Seul-Coeur, they always knew it would be a risk. The town's population was secretive, and they had good reason to be. The first time they considered this invitation was shortly after Paul's visit, and it took them three years to decide at last to do it.

"Jean-Marie had doubts about the plan from the moment he read that Pauls died." They had never been enthusiastic, aware of the cultural pressure toward silence, but also knowing that openness could prevent a catastrophe. I need to know what kind of catastrophe he's talking about, what secrets are hidden in Seul-Coeur that makes everyone here so paranoid and venomous.

"I couldn't threaten anyone, Pierre," I say as I look up at him.

"Many people in this town do not believe that. It is a matter of who you are. Because of those distrustful people, you took a risk in coming here. Because you are from outside, I took a risk in bringing you here. Jean-Marie made clear to me this morning. *That* risk has not paid." I ask Pierre to sit down, and when he doesn't move, I order him to sit down. He slinks away from me to the shadows of his front porch entrance, embarrassed, ashamed at how he is behaving. At least he understands what it means for a man to stand over a woman who has nowhere else to go. He apologizes, but it will take a lot for me to forget the moment when this strange man became all too typical. I ask again what he is hiding, what the town is hiding, the nature of his risk in bringing me here and my risk in coming here, just how unsafe it is for me in Seul-Coeur. But he continues to make excuses, and then mutters something in his native tongue that is no more than gibberish to me. Finally I give up and return to my room.

Night has fallen again. If Seul-Coeur and Pierre won't give me answers when I ask for them, it might be time to take them. Lit by my cell phone, I load a small backpack with everything I think I'll need to investigate whatever is happening in the forest. A canteen of water, a few cans of food, an opener, a fork. A full can of bug repellent, because blackflies in the forest apparently travel in swarms large enough to be fatal. My iPad, which I've loaded with scans of official maps of the area, and the maps my father made during his visit and from his memory. A couple of paper maps in case my iPad battery dies. How accurate any of these maps are, I have no idea. There's the compass I bought at an outdoorsman's store in Boston so I can actually work out where I am. And dad's journal, a useless totem, something of him that I can keep with me no matter what I encounter in the forest.

Pierre knocks on the door of the den, asking if I can talk, but I say nothing. I wait until he says he's going to bed, and will talk to me in the morning. I don't move again until the light from the crack between my door and the floor disappears. Now the house is in darkness, and after waiting a few more minutes for Pierre to go to sleep, I step into the hallway. I'm glad he keeps his hinges oiled, as nothing is worse than sneaking out of a house with squeaky doors, not only for the risk of discovery, but also for the awful embarking-on-a-mystery cliché it invokes. I lace up my boots and zip my jacket, glad that at least I've come here in July, when I can be sure I won't freeze to death in a Canadian winter.

I've never seen the ground illuminated solely by moonlight before, its stolen light tinting the world a faded blue. It's just ordinary moonlight, but I've spent my life under the electric burn of city lights, and the moon all on its own is something strange to me. My path to the forest takes me past Pierre's abandoned barn, and the door looks to be ajar. I tug on it with my finger, and the entrance easily gives way.

When I step inside, the stench is the first thing to hit me—blood and rotting flesh. The barn is far from abandoned. Half a moose lies torn open and dismembered on the floor, ripped open at the belly, but with no organs heaped on the ground where I expect they'd have spilled out. Its antlers are worn down almost to stumps, and a fine powder covers the ground near the animal's head. When I kneel down and rub some of the powder between my fingers, I can feel that it's the same consistency as the stump. Whatever consumed the moose's guts and organs also made powder out of the antlers. The barn is dark, the moonlight only creeping in through cracks in the roof, but there is one sliver of blue illuminating enough of the moose's visage that I can see empty, bloody tunnels where its eyes once were.

If I was going to run back to Pierre's house and wait there until he could escort me back to Boston where I could numb myself to everything that's happened over the past week, it would be now. This would be the only sensible time to unpack everything I put in my amateur survival kit, go to sleep, and write off the entire experience as a nightmare averted. But this is Pierre's home too, and whatever mutilated this moose is part of the secret he's keeping from me. Maintaining the secret does me more harm than good. It's true that he may have taken a risk in bringing me here, but he doesn't think of the risk I took in coming here. If this could happen at Pierre's farm, then I'm no safer in his guest bedroom than in his barn—or even in the forest, for that matter. My father's journal—even though it sounds more hallucinatory than lucid in almost every line—is a better guide to this town than Pierre has been so far. This journal may be written by a madman, but I can trust the ravings of the author. I can no longer say that about Pierre.

I leave the moose in the barn. It's too late for him. The forest eats the moonlight, assimilating it into rifts of collapsed darkness. A faint, asynchronous clacking can be heard in the distance, coming from every direction at once. I am absorbed into the shadows of the trees.

4.

No matter how well I hide myself, Maschinot still finds me. What kind of horrible sensations does he experience that he can track me wherever I go? I've concluded that he will find me in these woods. It's inevitable. He has my trail, my scent, and that deceitful dog may kill me yet unless I can kill him first.

I don't know how long I was wandering in the forest. It's a simple task of orienteering to stay on a particular path if you keep a major feature like a lake on one side of you all the time. But I often found myself wandering into the nooks and crannies of the shoreline, waking up each morning from a fitful sleep that disoriented me. The otherworldly crimson and violet of the night forest kept me in a strange sort of sleep limbo. My closed eyelids were suffused with cold fire, the intensity of a glowing computer screen. I found myself exploring featureless crags and coves in Lac du Monarque, my thoughts jumbled, filled with insignificant distractions, even though I could feel my muscles wasting away. I gave no thought to eating, even as I grew weaker and eventually unable to lift my knapsack thanks to the weight of its cans of food. One evening as the sun set I pried open each can and wolfed down every morsel of beans without even bothering to build a fire. It had been two days, maybe even three, since I ate anything. I had no time to cook, no time to eat, when the battle with Seul-Coeur lay ahead. But the town was fighting me already. As I vomited my meal of seven cans into the silent waters of the lake, I understood why my thoughts were obscured—a single moment of clarity in those days in the forest. The town itself didn't want to be found.

Yet I found the town. I could see its sad excuse for a skyline sticking out from the layers of trees at sunset. There was a farmhouse, still distant from the town, far enough away that it might be abandoned or at least neglected. It might be a place where I could rest away from those lights, even though their patterns appeared violently whenever I closed my eyes. There might even be something I can eat inside, I thought. My strength was failing me now, my muscles weak and in constant pain. That vampiric town had bled me of my energy. But I could rest, and I fell asleep on a mound of dust and mud, curling up in the corner of the barn. I don't know how long I slept, but I was woken by the creaking of the door, and an accented voice that was terribly familiar to me.

There was Maschinot. He was looking for someone, I was certain of it, but he kept casting his eyes around at his own level. If he noticed me on the floor, he never showed it. He still kept talking—in French, I think—as if he expected a response. I didn't know who else he was meeting in this barn in the middle of the night, but I wasn't about to stick around to find out. Before he could get out of my way, I was on him. I used the last of my strength to wrap my arms around his neck. My wild kicking managed to hit the back of his knee, and we rolled onto the floor together. It wasn't hard for him to free himself from me. My body's weakness was reasserting itself, though I'd never surrender to that liar. His clothes and hair were covered in hay from where I had tackled him to the ground, and I gathered I didn't look much better.

"Pauls! What are you doing? How did you get here?" How I got there was none of his business. All that mattered was that I was there, and that Seul-Coeur wouldn't keep its secrets from me for much longer. "Pauls, you should not ave come. You need rest an you need help. It is dangerous for you here." But Maschinot can't threaten me! I'm bringing down his town and his secrets and conspiracies. I could hear him calling after me, shouting my name as I fled into the darkness. He'll never find me until I want to be found. And then I'll have him.

* * *

Even in the hottest days of the year, the darkest times of night are still cold. I'll need at least a couple of hours of sleep tonight if I'm going to find anything in the morning, but I have to put as much distance between Pierre's farm and myself before he notices I'm missing. That likely won't be until morning. The space disorients me, though. The jumbled corridors between trees twist and spiral around each other, leaving me unsure of whether I've been turned around. I feel as if my eyes are useless because of the way the darkness eats light. Then a flicker appears, a purplish crimson that's become familiar to me in the few days I've spent around these woods. Its light isn't for human eyes, but by it, I can see.

I know my heart should beat harder than it has in its life, that its rhythm should overpower my ears, but it beats just as it would if I was on an ordinary nature walk. In fact, because I am able to find my way in this forest wavering with intermittent light, the strain might even be less than when I visit the hiking trails outside of Boston. The reddish-purple glow of the trees is lighting my way, but as I look into the distance, the light gives nothing away. At maybe fifteen feet from me the light doesn't diminish anymore. It just stops, like it has its own boundary or skin. The compass keeps me oriented in the right direction while I lead the light instead of it leading me.

Daylight is still about three hours away, if that time zone app is worth anything. These scruffy hiking boots are definitely worth something too in a mess of roots, trees, and marshes three inches deep with mud at one step and three feet deep at the next. Every time I have to steady myself on the terrain, my hands brush or crush at least three insects. They are never not squirming. But I know the route to the crash site. I have a map of the terrain in pdf and paper, with four days' worth of canned food and a brand new $20 can opener.

The light keeps me safe. Sometimes I stop walking so I can restore my energy for a farther trek, and the tree-lights stop with me, waiting for me to continue. My father's journal described the lights of Seul-Coeur as a terrible illumination, as if the needles of the trees were glowing with white-hot energy and slowly forcing themselves deeper into his eyes. It's only now that I understand, in these small hours of the night amidst trees glowing like backlit blood, that dad never really expected to find answers about mom here. We only ever discover what we expect to find. Dad had convinced himself that Seul-Coeur was the center of an evil presence, an unnatural part of the world. Everything in his journal bears it out. For so long, whenever I tried to help him, he turned me away. Not once did he ever tell me to go away. He was crueler than that. Simply telling me to piss off would have been an act of mercy. Instead, he turned away the people who wanted to help him by making that help ineffective. He would fake interest in other people from time to time, but that was just to humor Aunt Danielle and me. He would always revert to his obsessions and isolation until giving up was the only sensible option left. I could never have saved him from himself. Dad came here expecting to die.

My father was filled with fear at every moment of his time here. The scribbles in his journal show that he was barely keeping himself together—and that was just the state of his handwriting. Before I came here, the stories could only have been hallucinations. I see flickers of sunlight through the tops of the trees, and when I roll over to face the sky after having tripped over a broken tree branch, I watch the deep red lights, my phantom night-time companion, receding into the murky hue of dawn. I hoist myself up and sit on the dew-covered ground with my back to a tree. Its dying blush, like the warm glow of a flashlight pressed against skin, envelops me and I rest my eyes for just a moment.

* * *

Darkness has legs.

A thousand legs jutting in all directions from segmented bodies wriggling like worms—and the sound emanates from everywhere, from each tree and leaf. I can even hear the noise crawling across my hands. Click. Clackclack. Click, cleck… clack. It's useless to try to replicate the sound in writing. The tempo is erratic, the variations impossible to represent with human phonemes and characters. Perhaps the sound is like a Geiger counter, a sign of the radiation that I'm certain is withering me. I've been wasting away for days now, though I have no idea how long it's really been. Those satanic forest lights obscure the sunrise and sunset—those lights—the chaos of that clacking—it consumes me. It can only be some trap to convert me to just another hollow husk rotting on the forest floor, home to those eleven-legged spiders and polygonal beetles I've seen crawling among this absurd plant life.

I can feel Maschinot's presence everywhere in these woods. I know he's hunting me, and I'll be ready for him—provided that the emaciating light doesn't waste me first. Or the worms. I can see them wriggling and inching underneath the ground, emitting a blue glow that radiates through the soil and the grass. I try to match the clacking sounds to their movements, but every time I think I've figured out how a particular sound is related to a particular motion of the worms, they jump out of rhythm again. I'm terrified that the worms will discover I'm here. Once that happens, it'll be simply a matter of time before they emerge from the ground, wrap me in the centipede tentacles of their legs and drag me under the earth to suffocate in a shallow grave. That meeting in Shawinigan was nothing more than a trap to lure me into this alien nightmare.

For days I've consumed nothing but rainwater and my own sweat, enough to keep me alive. At last I've come to a clearing, a huge gap in the trees. It's afternoon—I can work that out from the position of the sun—and the heat is growing unbearable now that I'm out of the shade. The only trees in this clearing are dead and collapsed. Even the grasses and mosses that feed on the decay are unhealthy.

The land itself has been scarred, traumatized, and all life here is without an anchor, a foundation, left to drift until death. This can only be the crash site. The worms have disappeared, escaping deeper under the dermis of ground where their unearthly glow is hidden from view. With the departure of these creatures I have one less haunting to endure, but the question remains of where I will search, and what kind of evidence lingers. I've staggered to the center of the clearing now, where I see an outcrop of rock jutting out of the tangled growths of dead and dying grasses and weeds. I see an opening in the rock, a dark hole leading to a deep cave. Then a rustling noise in the distance, and my head jerks up, scanning for my predator. I can see the face of a man staring at me from the edge of the clearing, the same reddish-brown color as Maschinot, a complexion that must be common to this place. He darts behind a tree thinking I haven't seen him. So I shout as loudly as I can. "Maschinot! Come out and kill me like a man you son-of-a-bitch!" He steps into plain view out of the glowing darkness of the woods. He's a better hunter than his friend. Maybe Maschinot brought his acquaintance along as a distraction, someone to take hold of my attention so he could stealthily go in for the kill. But instead, my predator walks out into the clearing.

"Pauls… please…" His hands are up above his head, and I don't know what kind of trick he'll try to pull on me. "You are not well. You are in this woods for almost a week. Let me take you to a doctor. I can help you." I walk toward him. I don't know how the branch got into my hand, but as I send it crashing into his head I'm glad it's here. His arm blocks most of the blow, and I'm weak from the forest sapping my energy, but I still manage to knock him to the ground. Maschinot is dazed now, and his friend is running toward me. I won't give these murderers the satisfaction of killing me like they killed the people on that plane. God knows how many others have died by getting too close to this town's secrets. I'll wait for them in the cave, in darkness. Then we'll see who's really weak.

* * *

Shafts of sunlight streak through the trees and awaken me. I've only slept for a few hours, according to my watch, but it's daylight now, and as I groggily open my eyes I wonder why I'm so comfortable sleeping on ground. As I look around me, I'm about a foot off the ground, hovering. Every hair on my body extends out in static waves from my skin, and my scalp is a mass of soft tinsel. I'm kept afloat by a strange bubble of electricity, an electromagnetic field that can somehow undo the Earth's gravity.

I grab hold of a tree root to pull myself down to the dirt, then stand up and sling my bag onto my back. There's no time to reflect on the strangeness of my sleeping arrangement. It's daylight, and it's warm, and since it isn't even noon yet I know it's going to get hot. I have to put as much distance as possible between myself and where Pierre might be before mid-afternoon, when the summer heat of this place gets too thick to move. Sweat already beads on my forehead, and it will only get worse. I consult my compass, then my map (both paper and electronic versions). Even though there are weird peaks of static electricity around, my iPad still works well, and it doesn't take me long to work out my route to the crash site. After all that's happened in the two weeks since dad's funeral, *this*—right here, right now—is the only purpose I have. As to how I'll get out of Seul-Coeur and back to my life in Boston when "this" is all over, I haven't a clue. I have to put that kind of anxiety out of my mind if I'm going to stay focused.

While sauntering on, I think about the highlighted places in my father's journal where he was lucid enough to describe accurately what was around him, and as I trek through the forest these descriptions become manifested in reality. I stop to watch a long, huge insect crawl along the branch of a tree. It's the size of something I'd expect to see in the Amazon, not in a place that goes through a real winter. The thing is the size of a wriggling, writhing tube of toothpaste, and as it squirms down the branch it doesn't move in a straight line. Instead, it curves and spirals its segmented body, wrapping itself around the wood like the pattern of a black candy cane. Its hundreds of armored legs keep a tight grip on the tree as it approaches a leaf, which it then eats in quick bites with a mouth that seems to have several jaws.

When I reach the crash site, it's become so humid that my sweat won't even evaporate. I can't cool off, but I can't dehydrate either. My jacket has been wrapped around my waist by its sleeves since I woke up this morning, but now even the black stripes of my shirt attract more solar heat to my body than I can take. Yet through it all, my attention is clear. I'm walking on the ground where my mother died.

The trees here are shorter and thinner, all younger than the ones surrounding the oval would-be field. I got here by finding the remnants of a path the forensic investigation team plowed through the brush. That path, and most of the crash site itself, has been grown over with bushes, ferns, and grasses, but the plants aren't yet so thick that I can't navigate through them. There are thickets of small yellow flowers growing in irregular patches over where the plane must have come down.

Between these flowers and the natural erosion of the soil into a gradual sinking slope, any scar of the plane's impact has been long healed. Even so, I almost lose my balance stepping on loose, muddy ground as I walk down the incline. My reflexive groping on the bank uproots a handful of flowers, and I examine them once I stand at the bottom of the overgrown scar among waist-high misshapen blades of supersized grass. The flowers have none of the regularity of any flower I've seen. The blossoms are of different sizes and shapes, each petal varying even on the same flower, and no two flowers are patterned the same way. As I explore the brush, more of the same. Flowers and grasses and insects are all strange, just like so much of what I've seen in the town. So many are crooked, irregular, bent out of any semblance of a proper form. But that's all they are. Just more examples of irregularity. I can record as many of them as I want, take as many measurements of the impossible angles of petal shapes or zigzagging blades of grass, or how long the distended mouth of that praying mantis is. But none of these details will tell me anything about how they got that way. The forest gives me no more of an explanation than

Pierre or anyone else in this town ever did. Even the forest betrays its promises.

That's when I hear the clacking. It's faint at first, but then… I know that stutter well now, that rhythm that's barely rhythmic at all, a noise that slowly makes every other sound that might occur—birdsongs, winds, the chirping of insects, my own voice—fade into insignificance. I slip back into the trees, hoping to escape it, my legs tangled in vines and bushes as I avoid the easier paths that were once well-worn. This time the clicks follow me, a noise without a source, a voice without a speaker. The noise comes from the air itself, echoing in space too full of obstructions for echoes to resonate. The clacking vibrates the trees like tuning forks, and I can sense in layers of sound my drumming heartbeat, my panicking legs jumping over bushes whose crooked thorns threaten to cut through my jeans and into the flesh. At long last I reach a clearing where I can get my bearings. The clacking seems more distant now, as if it stays at the borders of the clearing. I take a few readings from the compass and determine my location on my paper map, at least roughly. But I can hear the clicking grow faster, chaotic patterns overlapping and reverberating. Irregular rises and falls in pitch and tempo steal my thoughts away. There's a rocky outcrop in the middle of the field that looks to be a small cave, a place where I can escape the sonic assault.

Dad's journal mentioned a cave at scattered points in the entries during and after his time here. But nothing was coherent enough for me to decipher. Those entries were written at his most unstable times, and when I read them, they were more like nightmares come to life than memories or experiences. I duck inside and enter the nightmare.

* * *

Each of them had a thousand claws and all those limbs were made of darkness enclosing me in a thick blanket of humidity. Every pore of my body, every cell of my flesh, was filled with black scratching. I do not remember when I woke up, but only that when there was light again a middle-aged woman was patting my forehead with a cloth. She spoke thick, incomprehensible French. I could feel the voices—my skin could pick up sound like an eardrum. It was excruciating. A voice that sounded like Maschinot's faded in from outside my field of vision. Merci, Jeannette, merci. All I can see are blurs and openness and colors fading and blending with each other, colors I've never seen before. Are these inhuman colors the only ones I will see from now on? Only colors without shapes. The darkness took my sight away. The Maschinot voice asks in English how I feel. I don't know *how* I feel, but I can feel. Pauls, do you remember? I remember Pauls, many Pauls. One of those Pauls hugged his daughter when she was a little girl. Another of the Pauls desperately wanted to during those years when she was in college and running away from him because of Zoiey. There was another of the Pauls who loved Zoiey, but I couldn't see Zoiey anymore. What did they do with Zoiey? Zoiey died, that was all. But I can't believe the Maschinot voice telling me this. These words don't make any sense. There's a Paul out there with Zoiey. I remember that Paul. Can you help me find him? Where is he? The voice turns away and I can't see the reddish color anymore. Please help me find her. Please help me. I just want to hold her again. It's been so long. Almost as long as we were together. Why did you take her away? Pauls, I am so sorry. Maschinot? Was that you? I am here, Pauls. I am here to help you. Why is she gone? Why is she gone? Because she is gone, Pauls. I am sorry. Here. I will dry your eyes for you. The cloth scratches. We don't always know what happens in the cave. Jean-Marie spend long time in the cave trying to find you. He sleeps in my room. Maschinot and the woman speak in French again, and I think she's left. Can you hear me Maschinot? He says yes, and I ask him where he was, what the claws were, what that darkness was. I could feel the darkness. Darkness isn't something you can feel. Les Bêcheux, he called them. The Diggers. You can feel their darkness. I felt their darkness many times. Their darkness, it comforts me, because I visit them since I am a child. Their darkness is our heritage, our birthright. You are too old to feel it. Your brain, your mind, it is not custom to the Diggers. The darkness try to talk with you, but the words of darkness snap you. An old man's brain is not plastic. I don't understand. I know, Pauls. What did they do to Zoiey? Nothing at all. I am so sorry.

* * *

Blackness. I can feel blackness. I remember the mouth of the cave, how the browning grass made the land around it almost desert-like, the forest's scar. It was panic and confusion that took me here. Even my thoughts were in pieces. They *are* in pieces. Now I lie on grass, and it's sunset. I can feel the sunset, and I dig fingernails into my face to scrape photons away from my skin, to test if the sun collapsed to a tiny pulsar and hid in my mouth.

"Marilyn! Marilyn! Can you see me? Can you see me?" My hand is on his face, and I ask if this is Pierre. He whispers "Yes, yes! But not wit your ands. Can you see my face wit your eyes?" He pants desperately and holds his face only inches above mine. I want to scream at him to get away from me, but my voice is caught in a vacuum.

"My glasses, can you see their shape? Can you see my eyes under my glasses?" I blink and shake my head with convulsive speed. The frames of his glasses are round, thick black plastic, slightly flatter on the top. And his eyes are behind his glasses, a deep brown with a hint of red that never appears in a human's eyes. He asks me if I can stand, and I don't know. "Well, know fast. We have a way to walk."

"Who took me?" Pierre doesn't know what I mean. He takes my hand, helps me stand up, and holds me steady while I test the muscles in my legs. My legs are phantoms, unsure if they still touch the Earth. "The cave. The last thing I remember, I was in the cave. There was darkness that ate light, engulfed the beam from my flashlight. My bag.

Where's my bag?!" But Pierre has it slung around his shoulder, and tells me everything is in it: food, iPad, maps, journal.

"I couldn't find the flashlight," he says. "It must be back in the cave."

"The cave… who took me?" He still doesn't know what I mean. But we're walking now, slowly out of the clearing. "I was in the cave. Something touched me. And then I don't remember. Who took me out of the cave?" He says it was mammair, but that's a French word I still don't know.

"My mother."

—But he told me he'd lost his mother. I ask Pierre again who took me out of the cave, yet he just tells me to keep walking, that we have to reach his truck and get out of Seul-Coeur, that people are coming for us. I'm covered in mud, and dirt is packed so tightly under my fingernails that I can feel it wedging apart my cuticles. My eyes are still dazzled from being in a lighted world again, and Pierre has to guide me through the spiraling twists of the clearing's dying grass, then under the canopy of the trees again. I thought Pierre was coming after me. I can see there have been tears flowing down his cheeks for a long time, and he can only say he's sorry over and over again. Jean-Claude is coming, he says, and he's not alone. The mob killed Jean-Marie's wife that morning, and they may have killed Jean-Marie already, too. At this, I shove him away from me and he falls over a rock, flailing into a bush.

"Marilyn, please! We have to go!" he shouts from his supine position on the branches.

"You told me I'd be safe here! You told me I'd have answers about my father and my mother! Then you tell me nothing and threaten me and now that thug pilot kid is leading a lynch mob after me!?"

He staggers to his feet with a hand outstretched in a defensive position, pleading. "I promise I will tell you evryting when we are a safe distance away. They kill my two best friends and they will kill us too. Please!"

I ask more than once if what he says is true, and Jean-Claude's gang really did kill the mayor's wife Jeannette, who used to go camping with Pierre when they were children, skinny-dipping in Lac du Monarque on humid summer days. I can see straight again, and the sun will set soon, so I offer him my hand and we run through the woods as fast as we can to reach his truck. Pierre says that if they catch up to us, at least we'll be better able to defend ourselves there, where he's left his hunting rifle. I ask why he never brought it with him, if he knew Jean-Claude may ambush him.

"I knew you would be frightened. You don't trust me. For good reason, you don't. But I need you to trust me now."

The sun has turned bright pink when we reach the dirt road along the lakeshore, not far from where Pierre hid his truck. Suddenly my shadow is scorched into the ground in front of me in a burning gaze of headlights. When I turn around I see the profile of a truck, its beams of light obscuring the faces of the people inside. Crammed shoulder to shoulder in the flatbed are the silhouettes of five men holding crowbars, chains, and other makeshift weapons.

5

The sun still peeks above the treetops, and the headlights are shining only to blind and disorient us. Yet I can see something obscuring their beams, moving over the edge of the lights. Jean-Claude steps out of the truck and shouts something in French, a scream that's also a rasping growl. He holds a knife, and sparks of electricity jump back and forth from the blade to his body. Pierre steps in front, as if to shield me from an inevitable assault. He casts a quick glance of reassurance at me, but he can't hide that he's terrified.

The others jump to the ground from the truck's flatbed, but stay by the vehicle as if waiting for a signal. Jean-Claude nods to the man still occupying the passenger seat, and the headlights switch off. Jean-Marie, the mayor, is tied to the truck's radiator grill, half his scalp ripped off his head, blood from the wound hardened over his face. His legs, below the knee, are ragged stumps of protruding bone fragments and dangling flesh, having been dragged along the road under the front bumper for many miles. I step backwards, wondering if I can survive a leap into the cover of the woods. But the trees are on the other side of the dirt road, too far away for us to get there quickly. The man holding the rifle grips it by the barrel, wrings his hand around the cylindrical metal as if hesitant to shoot. While I try to figure out which of the lynch mob we might be able to knock out first, Pierre and Jean-Claude are shouting at each other in French. Pierre is pleading, almost prostrate before him, but Jean-Claude laughs at him, his voice nothing but rage and contempt. The boy slices off the top of Jean-Marie's ear. The beaten man tries to scream through the gag in his mouth, but he's barely alive to muster the breath.

I can't tell if I scream because any noise I might make is drowned out by a sudden onslaught of clacking, faster and louder than any of the clicking noises heard in the forest. The sounds assault me now, and even Jean-Claude is afraid. But Pierre is beaming, smiling as it charges out of the forest, releasing a howl infested with clicks—a staccato machine-gun of many different pitches at once. The forest explodes with bright crimson light that overpowers the dying rays of sunset, and a torrent of water spirals up from the surface of the lake, exploding out in a mushroom cloud to drench us all. The creature is enormous, moving so fast it nearly flashes past me. Its exterior is black and has the tough exoskeleton of an ant, but the hard skin is flexible, and its long body is segmented like a worm, undulating back and forth as it zips past me on countless crab-like legs. I've seen creatures like these—not seen, but felt—as the innards of a cave, rigid as bone and supple as curdling blood. I can sense the creatures moving even now, just like when the darkness absorbed into their intestinal walls. But this creature is different. At its front, its body turns upward ninety degrees like a centaur, with two arms ending in five-fingered claws. They'd be like human arms if it weren't for the skin thick as ebony armor. Its head is hairless, large enough to match its huge body, and the exoskeleton is not completely black, but rather blends into coppery skin as it merges with the almost-human face of an elderly woman.

The mob that jumped from the truck's flatbed are all running toward the creature now, holding their weapons high. The man with the rifle releases a few rapid bursts, but the bullets hit the tough carapace of the creature's body, doing little harm. The multitude of legs she has are clearly attached to her skeleton, but they seem to move independently as they strike and stab her attackers in all directions. Her body flows back and forth like dragon dancers on Chinese New Year with a thousand mescaline trippers under the costume. A man falls face-down in front of me—a crunch of shattering bones as one of the creature's hind legs impales him from behind and into the ground through his abdomen. Three of the surviving men are attacking her at the front, where her body rises up vertically. Her movements are restricted by the body of her first dying attacker in which her spade-like foot is stuck. The piece of enervating meat at the end of the spade flops about as the creature attempts to free itself of the encumbrance by vibrating its leg like a jackhammer. Meanwhile, the man with the rifle stands back from the melee, waiting to get a clear shot at the creature's barely human face. I pick up the crowbar dropped by the dying man. Even dying, he looks at me with fuming hatred as he writhes and quakes on the end of the spade. His face demands that I die, and as he is finally released from the creature's foot and flung in my direction, I answer his hatred with one mid-air crowbar thwack that smashes a gaping fissure in his head.

I sneak along the shadow of the forest canopy towards the man with the gun. He's so captivated by his friends' fight with the creature that he no longer notices the person he came here to kill. He *does* notice me when my crowbar breaks his left kneecap, and he fires a shot uselessly into the ground while he tries to pivot toward me. He tumbles and knocks me onto the ground with him, but the rifle falls away from his reach. He grabs my belt, trying to drag me toward him, and I swing the crowbar haphazardly. One side of his face is caved in and blood is falling from his mouth. Yet he's still conscious, lurching forward to slash at my face with his hands like claws. But I have his rifle, and I'm not afraid of him anymore. He lies on his back now, his hands grasping at the gaping hole I've shot through his chest, as if he could gather the blood gushing from the tattered wound. All the mud around him is dark red when he finally slackens and deflates, ceasing the futile attempt to preserve his life.

Jean-Claude has turned away from Pierre, leaping on the prostrate, sobbing mayor to hack his body to pieces. The boy's scream doesn't just puncture my eardrums, but also the air itself. His arms and even his face seem to disappear into Jean-Marie's body along with the knife. Crimson lightning explodes from the mayor's shredded carcass and crawls jittering across the truck. Wherever the lightning crawls, strange bulbous growths suddenly appear on the vehicle, unnaturally organic bubbles of metal. The metal tumors take on a life of their own, distorting the truck into a crooked mass of lumps, radiating the same purple fire I've seen coming from the trees. Jean-Claude looks behind him and sees his friends falling limply from the blood-soaked creature, their bodies ripped and mangled with slashes and blows from its chitinous arms. The two howl at each other as Jean-Claude leaps onto the beast's face, his knife raised and searching for the sweet spot to land a killing blow. Even standing at a distance from them, I feel the metal of the rifle getting hot with static electricity, but I can't look away from the fight. His blade is embedded deep in the creature's eye socket, but the pain becomes a horrific screech of anger as one twisted mandible grabs him by the head and wrenches him away from her face. Jean-Claude is helpless now, suspended in midair kicking and punching, landing no blows, uselessly grasping for his knife again. She opens her mouth into a trapezoidal cavern filled with teeth before she brings him toward her face and tears through his neck. As she rips Jean-Claude away from her mouth, she's covered in his blood. Jean-Claude's head is attached to his body by only a flimsy rope of flesh, and streams of black fluid pulse from his neck hole in irregular jets. She throws him away—the jerkiness of the motion breaking the tenuous rope—and his body crashes into the truck's windshield while his head flies into the lake.

The creature is disoriented now, trying to get a grip on the butt of the knife protruding from its eye. Then I see Pierre. There's one member of the mob left alive, sitting on top of Pierre's back at the shallow edge of the lake. Pierre is fighting his attacker but failing, unable to get a solid grip on any part of his body, running out of energy as he drowns in six inches of water and mud. I walk across the field of bodies, past the creature who whimpers as her black, bony fingers probe and grabble her wound. The man drowning Pierre only turns around when he hears the clack of a round being loaded into the rifle's chamber. I feel my whole body flinching as my bullet blasts through his head, and he falls off Pierre into the muck. I put the rifle down to haul my friend out of the water now polluted with cranial fragments, and I pull him up into the open air.

He's still gasping. His face, hands, and clothes are spattered with blood and bone. He assures me that none of it is his. I help him to stand, but as he sees the gore around him, he almost collapses again to his knees. He staggers toward the creature, who kneels on the ground to embrace him with her strange, multi-jointed arms. Her voice is still riddled with clicking sounds and the guttural distortions of her mutated throat, but I can tell now that she's speaking Pierre's tongue. He's incapable from shock of making a complete sentence, but I can understand the word he keeps saying to the creature: "Mammair, mammair." Mother.

Half an hour later we reach Pierre's truck, parked in the place where he, Jean-Marie, and Jeannette used to hang out and pass the hours away when they were teenagers. In that very same spot by the edge of the lake, we stop to wash the blood and mud off our faces and clothes in the lapping waters. Although it is dark now, the waving crimson lights of the trees accompany us, along with the creature, who keeps a respectful distance as if she was a chaperone on her son's first date. As Pierre pulls himself together, he is able to introduce me to his mother, Hélêne. It was her generation who first made contact with the Diggers, the aliens who found themselves stuck on Earth by accident, waiting patiently in the forest by Seul-Coeur for the ride back to their homeworld. The aliens have a strange sense of time, according to Pierre. Apparently a wait of five hundred years is as inconsequential to them as I'd find a slightly annoying wait for the bus in rush-hour traffic. As far as he can figure out, there may be another dimension of time that's invisible to us, and that only becomes perceivable when you spend long enough in their caves. He asks if I had a sense of time while in the caves, and my memories are strange and fragmented, but it feels as if days went by as I wandered that tunnel. The Diggers' caves aren't only in the space between rocks, but are woven into the space between atoms, between protons and neutrons, between quarks. They live in the dimensions where space curls up into twisted, spiraling loops. Whether I was in there for two hours, two weeks, or two millennia, I cannot say.

I wait in Pierre's truck while he says goodbye to his mother. She's a monster to me, a freakish hybrid of human and Digger. But blood still drips from the wound in her eye, and her almost-human face grimaces with pain. Encircled by the red light from the trees, I see them embrace, and can make out in their silhouette a huge segmented arm—more inexplicably flexible than her exoskeleton would allow— stroking her son's head. Pierre leaves her embrace, returning to the truck, and his mother dives back into the forest faster than I'd have ever thought a creature her size could move. But I thought any and all creatures her size died sixty-five million years ago. Though out of sight, the violet residue of her presence flutters in the branches of the trees. There are new legends brewing, newly budding folk tales walking these fluorescent forests.

We are silent as Pierre first climbs into the driver's seat. Then Pierre tells me through tensed lips that the dirt road along the lakeshore is the only way back to the highway. We will have to drive back past the scene of our fight with Jean-Claude and his posse. Before he can start the truck, he rests his head against the steering wheel, the skin of his face pulled tighter than I have seen it before. Each of his breaths takes immense effort. He looks more human than ever.

At last, Pierre has composed himself enough to start the engine. It doesn't take us long to reach the scene of the fight, but once there, we find nothing. Jean-Claude, the lynch mob, and what was left of Jean-Marie have all disappeared. There's only the teratomatic heap that was once the mob's truck, mutated out of anything like its intended shape, its wheels and windows encrusted with metal tumors. Doors are growing out of its roof, strange branches and facsimile tires out of its doors. We drive on, but I ask where the bodies are. Pierre says that cleanup has already begun, but I have no need for cryptic statements and secrets anymore. And so he explains everything. Or at least he explains everything that he can explain.

The people of Seul-Coeur weren't as naive as an outsider might think, and when creatures as strange as the Diggers crash-landed in a tornado of light—setting off impossible magnetic phenomena—the townsfolk knew that they were not of this planet. A few of the elder generation went insane, believing the apocalypse had begun, but they were all devoured by old age within five years, so their backward attitudes would be no problem for the town moving forward. Only the children were able to talk to the Diggers at first, because children's brains are more plastic, and could absorb the dislocating effects of the caves without any serious mental disturbance. The Diggers experience spatial reality quite differently from humanity. They don't *see* light, but rather *sense* it. Neither English nor French, according to Pierre, has a word that can accurately describe the sensation. When he was in university, Pierre took a biology course where he learned that some species of fish can detect electrical charge patterns in the ocean, and he's pretty sure the Diggers' electromagnetic sense works something like that. But he can't be sure, because his mother and the other hybrids have never been able to recount their perceptions in human language. The people of Seul-Coeur discovered what the Diggers were because their children had been able to bridge the communication barrier.

The Diggers were able to decode human culture as they approached our star system, listening to the radio waves we sent into space. Because most of the transmissions they encountered were echoes of the Second World War, they were wary of us. There are some species of ant that are utterly peaceful, and that only kill other ants if they are from more invasive ant species, or if an ant from their own colony has become infected with a virus or a spore, and threatens the health of the entire community. These, according to the Diggers, are the only reasons ever to kill—not for sport, profit, resources, and tribalism, which is how the Diggers understand all human politics. As they approached Earth, they decoded more and more transmissions of our wars, and became terrified of these flesh-based organisms who built death camps, starved some cities, scorched others, and created what they called "stars of the instant." Nuclear bombs.

The first humans the aliens were able to talk to were curious children like Hélène Maschinot, who had wandered out into the woods and weren't afraid of the darkness within the Diggers' newly built caves. The Diggers found hope in her, and made the people of Seul-Coeur an offer: they would teach the humans about their species. They would show the humans how to perceive electromagnetism as the Diggers did, a kind of listening touch—or tactile hearing—that lets them channel and shape pure energy. In return, they asked to be taught particular aspects of human existence. Although they found our visual sense laughably limited, they were intrigued by it, and wanted to know how we perceived the universe as if it was a two-dimensional map. They wanted to learn about human history and genealogy, to discover how we developed our skill for destruction while refining our sense of curiosity—our most redeeming feature, according to the Diggers. Pierre had no idea how successful his people were at learning the Diggers' lessons, but he got the impression that the Diggers were satisfied.

There were some concessions to be made, though. Fully understanding the perceptions of the Diggers and the strange geometry of the intra-space where they lived would require physically altering the human body, introducing cellular agents that would transform a human into a creature that was no longer human, but not fully Digger either. Hélène was the first of many to begin the hybridization process. The procedure began when she was fifteen years old. Pierre wasn't born until she was twenty-two.

We reach Pierre's farm and find it utterly destroyed. The house and the barn are both smoldering wrecks. The fire had mostly burned itself out, with only a few embers and glowing shards of timber left to be extinguished. I don't know how long we sit there with the hum of the engine as the only noise, Pierre gazing at the desolation with a cryptic, featureless expression, as if he had lost something very important, but also stood to gain. Soon enough, time lapses forward and we're on the road again.

"Time lapse" is not the correct description. It is an approximation to explain how time flows differently for me now, more asymmetrically than it had before I entered the cave—sometimes faster, sometimes slower. Maybe I became able to sense some kind of second or third dimension of time. One day, I might even be able to understand what that means.

Yet the sensation is unmistakable. Something has begun in me. Something similar to Pierre, to the people of Seul-Coeur. Almost all of them have an electromagnetic sense, and most of them grow up with hopes to become hybrids themselves, able to perceive the world more completely, and experience authentically the curved and curled spaces where the Diggers make their homes. Pierre has a rudimentary electromagnetic sense, as the organs for it only develop fully when you reach Hélêne's stage of hybridization, at which point the remaining human cells become a residue, a lingering inconvenience. Wider human society didn't matter to most people from Seul-Coeur. Humanity was something to be tolerated, and it wasn't a piece of themselves they felt they could be proud of. That was the other part of Seul-Coeur's bargain with the Diggers: because of humanity's craving for violence, there was to be no contact with the wider human population, or at least as little as possible. They asked for Seul-Coeur to become invisible, to disappear from human society, and to use that anonymity to protect them from any humans who would attack, dissect, or destroy the colony. It was a small feat to transform the natural distrust of outsiders that any isolated small town tends toward, into the active desire to force them away. Last night, that desire went too far.

I ask Pierre what will happen now, and he tells me the Diggers will not tolerate what occurred today. His mother has no doubt communicated to the rest of the colony what Jean-Claude and his friends did to Pierre, her, me, and poor Jean-Marie and Jeannette. They offered the people of Seul-Coeur an experiment in growing beyond the petty concerns of humanity, our selfishness, and the creativity of our violence. The experiment has failed. The Diggers asked for isolation to protect their way of life, and found that isolation easily becomes a weapon. To them, humans have proven themselves creatures that will turn any tool into a means for annihilation—a monstrous transformation. Those in Seul-Coeur who have kept their promise to give up violence will be either welcomed into the caves to accelerate hybridization, or can live elsewhere and keep the secret. Those who the Diggers can no longer trust will be neutralized, just as we suppress a malignant tumor with chemotherapy and radiation. Tumors are what Jean-Claude and his posse became when they decided that Seul-Coeur could be best protected through murder. The hybrids now have the task of putting the rest down: their mothers, brothers, and friends will excise them like one ant destroying its incurably infected fellow. A thought can be diseased just as an organ or an animal can. Seul-Coeur will now truly cease to exist, and its name will be erased and forgotten.

I finally ask Pierre about dad. He sighs, because there's nothing left to prevent him from telling me. I've never seen anyone so sad to get to what he wanted so much. He asks me how far into the story I know. The caves. The journal stops when Pierre's mother had taken dad out of the cave, and Pierre himself carried dad back to his house, where Jeannette had been summoned to bring dad out of his delirium. After dad was stabilized, Pierre tells me that someone from town ordered him to be sure the old man didn't make it out in any way fit to lure others to follow him. But the week of starvation, dehydration, heatstroke, paranoia—and the caves themselves—had accomplished that work already. When they reached Shawinigan, Pierre was able to tease enough information out of dad to contact Aunt Danielle to come get her brother. It took a few days, but she did. She found dad alone on a picnic table in a public campground. She never saw Pierre. Dad was broken, wasted, a shadow of himself, and in those last three years of his life he deteriorated faster than he ever had before.

Pierre will get me to a plane bound for Boston, but says we can't go to the closest airport at Rouyn-Noranda. It's too small, too distant from everywhere else to get more than propeller plane service, and most importantly, too close to Seul-Coeur. Anyone left in town who opposed my coming would expect me to go there. Instead we go to a place farther away but with more intense security, a wealthier community with golf courses frequented by businessmen the world over—a paradisiacal melting pot in the outlands of an isolated backwater. Copper-skinned hicks from the back country won't even be let into town, Pierre says. We eat lunch on the balcony of a hilltop hotel in Shawinigan overlooking a valley with a vineyard on one side and a ski slope, green for the summer, on the other.

When I ask him—as we sit in this idyllic yet manicured setting— what caused the plane crash, it turns out to have been exactly as I assumed. The Diggers don't strike what would be a *potential* danger to them, only what's an *actual* danger. My mother was just flying on an airplane whose instruments were damaged by a random discharge of static electricity, during the times in the Diggers' autonomic cycle when the whole cave system is more reactive than usual. But a discharge that size is so rare that a plane had never passed through it before in the five decades since the Diggers came to Earth. Pierre's description of the electricity reminds me of what we went through on the plane from Montreal, and I tell him as much. Pierre scoffs. That was just Jean-Claude's malicious joke, he says. He had threatened Pierre when we reached the hangar, knowing I wouldn't understand, and his goal by summoning the lightning with his own internal energies was to frighten me off. Jean-Claude knew that if this attempt to open the town failed, no one would ever try to end Seul-Coeur's isolation again.

Yet I still don't understand why Pierre was so adamant about bringing my father back to Seul-Coeur. This is my last demand of him. Pierre took a deep breath. He explained how certain people in the town, particularly Jean-Marie, wanted to repair what had gone wrong, restore dad's ability to think. But when Pierre arrived in Boston only to stand in front of a coffin—validating the obituary that Jean-Marie had discovered in the online city newspaper—Pierre saw for himself that the lingering effects of dad's exposure to the caves had eventually killed him. Seul-Coeur people aren't Catholic like the rest of Quebec, he said, because their gods follow through on promises. Seul-Coeur people don't believe in forgiveness, only reparations. If a material harm is done, the material harm is repaired. If the harmed person dies, no one can do anything more. No substitute is good enough, and neither is a symbol, which is the most I could be as far as the townspeople were concerned.

Pierre hasn't fully answered my demand. "What do you mean that dad died because of his exposure to the caves?" Pierre looks at me with that same cryptic gaze I saw when he was staring at the smoldering ruins of his farm, as if there was a gain hidden among all this loss. He opens his mouth but pauses, choosing his next words carefully.

"It's like what I told you before. Older people, their minds are not plastic enough to be altered. He was under so much stress also, with heatstroke, dehydration, he had not eaten properly for days. In that state, the beginnings of the change would drive him mad. It begins with perceptions, so he would think them hallucination. I go to Boston hoping to repair him, to bring him back and put him on proper progress. But the changes were too much."

✳ ✳ ✳

His words—as well as his omissions—only made sense to me long after that day in Shawinigan, as I became accustomed to those slipping and sliding perceptions of time. A person doesn't walk through a space threaded into the curled dimensions of quarks and electrons where light becomes tangible and time becomes place without it changing her somehow. I find it funny now when Pierre comes to visit me in Boston. I tell him that he's checking up on my progress, and the joke always makes him uncomfortable, as if he's worried that I worked out what he really wanted from me and my father. Of course I worked it out, which is precisely why he has no need to worry. Neither I nor my father would have walked into the caves holding Pierre's hand. We stubborn Americans have to be pushed or tricked into going where we don't want to go. Pierre is a better trickster than he lets on.

He's spent the last three years tracking down others who fled Seul-Coeur, in the hopes of starting a community somewhere else, where they could pass as ordinary people. He tells me Oklahoma is his most likely candidate, in the isolated regions of their Tribal lands. Every time he visits I ask him who else from Seul-Coeur has joined him in the west. I am secretly anticipating the name Rejeanne, the one person from that town who was genuine and kind to me. But he never lets those details slip. Pierre only ever tells me what he thinks I need to know. I always give him a friendly drive to the airport when he leaves, wishing him good luck with his resettlement project, as I always do, because I know his experiment has failed before it even begins.

One day, when his community of nomadic hybrids has been established in Oklahoma, he will ask me to join him there. I will say no, and I always will. Even though he was able to explain the Diggers' morality to me, I know now that he never truly understood it because, if he did, he would not be so cruel as to visit Boston twice a year to monitor my progress as if it were a scientific experiment. He knows that my body, brain, and mind are changing because of those few hours I spent in the caves, hours that were also weeks. He made an unscheduled visit this week for Aunt Danielle's funeral. She lied to me too, never telling me the true progress of her Parkinson's disease, even as she was dying. Perhaps the unmasking of that last lie broke my own will to dishonesty. At a small table in an even smaller pub, Pierre and I sit down together, and I tell him the truth that he already knows.

The plane crash in 1997 was the horror where all of this began. He's surprised to hear me mention it, as if he had forgotten all about my mother. Jean-Claude—that hooligan who was only trying to protect the secret of the town as the Diggers wanted—inadvertently gave me the necessary clue to put it all together. When Pierre took me to Seul-Coeur, the electromagnetic field that the Diggers generate was weak. So when Jean-Claude channeled it to attack his own plane, all he could do was create a light show to frighten me. But my mother's plane flew over Seul-Coeur at the peak of the energy's fluctuation, so the field would have had enough energy, if manipulated in the right way, to bring down a large aircraft. Maybe all that was needed was one or two immature young men impulsive enough to think that violence was the best way to enforce isolation. Of course, that backfired because a plane crash brings large teams of police officers, federal bureaucrats, and forensic scientists in its wake to investigate precisely what caused it. Maybe the shame of committing such violence, only to produce the exact result he wanted to avoid, was enough to drive a young man to give up on his farm, learn more about the wider world, and convince him that old-fashioned isolation would no longer be enough to protect his home. Pierre can't hide the shame on his face when I say this, so he needn't admit anything. I don't want his confession.

He knew that anyone who enters the Diggers' caves would begin the process of hybridization, just like his mother, and just like him. When you can no longer maintain your isolation that protects you from the rest of the world, you reach out to make the world a safer place. His original plan—to keep Seul-Coeur isolated by creating fear of the unknown, fear of danger and violence—did not take into account the power of human curiosity, the fact that others would eventually come. Taking down a jet plane or rounding up a posse to kill the outsider doesn't protect you from violence. It just brings the violence closer. Another plan was born the day that Pierre realized his failure, a plan in which I am unwittingly and irrevocably involved.

My father was right to distrust Pierre, even though dad could never have understood why. That town and so many of its people broke his life long before he was ever exposed to the spiraling dimensions housed within the caves. Occasionally I can even talk to dad, as my time-slipping perceptions interact with events that have long gone by. Maybe I play some role in the hallucinations that drove him over the edge. Even though I can sometimes see the past, thanks to the gifts of the Diggers, I understand that it can't be changed. Dad died in that plane crash too, even if his body never landed in that field of twisted debris and scarred earth. The path that took him from cave to coffin was written into his nature when my mother's plane went down. I know now what I can change, and what I must accept.

Sometimes I miss my mom and dad, but not always.

 Adam Riggio is a Newfoundland-raised and Hamilton-based writer of fiction, plays, and non-fiction. Coming from his birthplace in St. John's to complete a doctorate in philosophy, he settled in Hamilton out of love for its friendly attitudes, the cultural cosmopolitanism of southern Ontario, and the (somewhat) affordable rent. He has published articles in *Environmental Ethics* and *Doctor Who and Philosophy*, and his first play debuts in Hamilton in November of 2014. Adam blogs at adamwriteseverything.blogspot.com, and tweets at @adamriggio.

BlankSpace Publications, based in London, Ontario, Canada, is an independent press run by a band of nomadic herbivorous huntsmen constantly on the lookout for stories to subdue, devour, and circulate. Visit www.blankspacep.com to check out our catalogue and other promotions. The dedicated editors at *BlankSpace* (who are paid for their services in turnips, pignuts, and other edible roots) thank you for supporting independent publication.